M...   *h*
she

Re   ,
is   e
est   o
pr   -
ol   e
alr   e
ma   t
Lu   d
ho   t
as   e
'ac   e
tu   g
res

NEVER TOO LATE

Never Too Late

by

Christina Courtenay

Dales Large Print Books
Long Preston, North Yorkshire,
BD23 4ND, England.

1761739

British Library Cataloguing in Publication Data.

Courtenay, Christina
    Never too late.

    A catalogue record of this book is
    available from the British Library

    ISBN   978-1-84262-858-4 pbk

First published in Great Britain 2010 by
DC Thomson & Co. Ltd.

Copyright © Christina Courtenay, 2010

Cover illustration © Jill Battaglia by arrangement with
Arcangel Images

The moral right of the author has been asserted

Published in Large Print 2011 by arrangement with
Pia Tapper Fenton

Dales Large Print is an imprint of Library Magna Books Ltd.

Printed and bound in Great Britain by
T.J. (International) Ltd., Cornwall, PL28 8RW

CHAPTER ONE

The time was close to midnight when Maude put her ear to the keyhole of her bedroom door. All appeared to be quiet. It was time to go.

She had been lying on her bed, fully dressed, for hours. Her small valise was packed and ready, hidden at the back of her wardrobe, and she had the only fortune she was ever likely to possess in her reticule – her late mother's diamond necklace. Maude had no idea how much it was worth, but the stones were fairly large and beautifully cut. It ought to provide a roof over their heads, she reckoned, at least until they had figured out how Luke was going to support them.

Luke Hexham. The mere thought of him was enough to make her heart leap with joy. Tall and handsome, with wavy brown hair and eyes as green as a summer meadow, he was everything she wanted in a man. The wonder of it was that he loved her, and he'd promised they were going to make a life for themselves, one way or another. Maude didn't care that they had to resort to an elopement because her stubborn father was set on a match between her and Luke's cousin Edward instead. The only thing that mattered was that they would be together.

She loved him more than life itself.

Moving silently across the room, illuminated only by the moonlight streaming in through the window, Maude fetched her valise and travelling cloak, and put on her bonnet. Her fingers shook with excitement and nerves, but she succeeded in tying the bow under her chin eventually. When she was ready, she went to the door and turned the handle as slowly as she could, just in case it squeaked.

The door would not open.

She tried again, applying more force this time, but the door remained stubbornly closed. Maude felt tendrils of apprehension crawling through her. Why wouldn't it budge? Was it jammed shut in some way?

Oh, dear God, why tonight of all nights? she wanted to howl.

She pushed against the wood with her shoulder, giving it an almighty shove at the same time as turning the handle, and hoped that the resulting thump wasn't too audible. She need not have worried.

'There's no point, Miss. Best just go back to bed,' she heard a sardonic voice say from outside. Her father's valet, Ryder. 'You won't be goin' nowhere tonight.'

Maude gasped, then swallowed a cry of anguish. They had been found out. Someone must have warned her father of the proposed elopement and he had locked her in, putting Ryder outside her door as an extra precaution.

But how could that be? No one knew, except for herself and Luke.

She stilled, the blood inside her turning ice-cold. Who could have told Sir Richard

Bellamy about his daughter's impending flight? Surely not Luke? No, that was impossible. He loved her and would never betray her. But who else was there? A sob tore out of her and she put a hand in front of her mouth to stop others from escaping. The last thing she wanted was to give Ryder the satisfaction of hearing her cry. He would no doubt relish telling her father about that.

Gritting her teeth against the pain of having her plans thwarted, she flung the cloak off onto the nearest chair and started to pace the room. The more she walked, the more she became convinced that the culprit had to have been Ryder. It made sense. She trusted Luke implicitly and if he'd wanted to cry off, he would have just said so. He had always been direct, never resorting to subterfuge. No – Ryder must have spied upon them. It was more than likely, he was forever creeping about the place. Maude shivered.

Damn the man! she thought, clenching her fists.

Either way, what did it matter who had

done the deed? The fact was that she was trapped here in her room, while Luke was no doubt becoming frustrated at having to walk the horses in the lane. He'd said he would wait for as long as it took, but if she did not appear before morning, he would know she was not coming.

And then what?

'Oh, Luke,' she whispered, tears streaming down her cheeks now. 'Come and help me, please!'

But he had no way of knowing that she needed his help – and she could not get word to him. Not with Ryder on guard and her room on the second floor. She was, indeed, going nowhere tonight.

She sank to the floor and gave way to despair.

CHAPTER TWO

'When are we leaving, Mama?' The child's repeated question caused Maude, Lady Hexham, to stifle a sigh.

'Soon, dearest. We must wait for your father's cousin's arrival.'

'How soon?'

Maude gritted her teeth in frustration. It was probably the tenth time her six-year-old daughter had asked the same questions in the last half hour, and Maude was ready to scream. She knew the situation was not of her daughter's making, however, as the real culprit was Luke, the new Lord Hexham. The man who was stepping into Maude's late husband's shoes.

The man who was taking everything.

Maude clenched her fists behind her back, battling to keep her emotions under control.

When she had first been informed of her husband's death a month earlier, she had felt nothing but relief, as theirs had not been a happy union. Fairly soon, however, the relief had given way to worry when she realised that he had left her and their child nothing. The estate was entailed and would go to his cousin, and there was apparently no widow's jointure for her. How was she to support herself and her daughter? And how could her father have agreed to such a disastrous marriage settlement on behalf of his only child? It beggared belief.

Never one to let adversity grind her down for long, Maude had tried to come up with a solution, but had hit on only two possibilities. She could throw herself and her child on the mercy of a distant cousin on her mother's side who was wealthy enough to be able to afford to take them in; or she could try to find a position as housekeeper. As long as her employers allowed her to keep her daughter with her, that was. The thought of living as a poor relation and being made to work for nothing did not appeal to her, however, so in the end she had reluctantly opted for the second choice.

Luckily she had kept the diamond necklace she had inherited from her mother, which, eight years ago, she had intended to take as her only dowry when she eloped. She had hidden it away, unable to even bear the sight of it because it reminded her of that awful night. Now it would come in useful once more and she had decided to sell it, in order to give herself time to apply for suitable positions. She could only hope the money would last.

'But why can't we stay here?' Anna's plaintive tone intruded on her mother's thoughts. The little girl was sitting on top of two small trunks, kicking her legs with monotonous regularity against their sides out of sheer boredom.

'Because this house belongs to the new Lord Hexham now and he will want his own family to live here.'

'We're his family, aren't we?' Anna looked

confused, her big emerald eyes, so like her uncle's, shiny with the threat of tears.

'In a way, yes, but…' Maud did not know how to explain to her daughter that Luke was hardly likely to view them with any charitable feelings. He had probably thought he'd never return at all, since his uncle had banished him from Hexham Hall some eight years previously because of the proposed elopement. Luke had apparently left in a huff, swearing never to set foot in the place again, and he had kept his word. Until now.

'Is he late?' Anna was still drumming with her heels and Maude longed to shout at the child to stop, but she knew that might set off the threatening tears and she did not feel able to deal with that at the moment. She had to somehow get through the ordeal of handing over the house, their home, to her former suitor.

'Yes, he is late. He has most likely been held up by the weather,' she told her daughter. It was raining stair rods, and claps of thunder reverberated round the hall every now and again. Still, Maude railed inwardly at Luke for not having the courtesy to arrive at the appointed hour. Surely he could have taken the weather into account? It was rapidly turning dark outside, and she and Anna had some distance to travel to the nearest inn before nightfall.

'Being late is rude, is it not?' Anna persisted, looking slightly smug that she was not at fault on this occasion.

'Yes, dear, unless there is a good reason.'

Just then, there came the sound of horses' hooves on the gravel outside the front door and the footmen rushed out to assist with the arrival of their new master. Inside, the butler Donne harried the rest of the household staff into a welcoming line behind Maude, who stood straight and took a deep breath, preparing herself to greet the new Lord Hexham.

The man she had once loved and lost.

She gave herself a mental shake. That was all a long time ago, and this was not the time to think of such things. It was in the past, forgotten. At least she assumed it was, by him. He'd never written so much as one letter; never enquired why she didn't keep their assignation. He obviously had not cared.

A veritable stranger swept into the hall on a gust of cold autumn air, shaking raindrops from his hat. He handed it to a footman, who stepped forward to take it together with his cloak. Maude stifled a gasp at the sight of the man before her – so easily recognisable, yet so changed from the youth she had once known.

Gone was the laughter and easy-going manner. Instead she saw a handsome but scowling countenance, darkened by the Spanish sun from his years in the Peninsula fighting the French. His eyes, as green as ever and fringed by dark lashes, were no longer twinkling, but serious and surrounded by tiny crow's feet, no doubt from squinting into that same sun. She noted that his shoulders were much broader, his body toned and muscled from years in the army. He had an air of assurance and authority, as if he was used to command.

Maude shivered, but took a deep breath and stepped forward.

'Welcome to Hexham Hall, my lord.'

He gave her a measuring stare, which she managed to return without quaking, and said, 'Thank you.'

He looked around the vast marbled hall, as if assessing the value of his newly acquired possessions. Maude was aware that the furnishings were somewhat shabby and the walls could do with a coat of paint, but she had not had the wherewithal to change that. Instead she had made sure it was all as clean as it could possibly be. The maids had been sweeping and polishing for days.

'I trust you will find everything in order. And now we shall leave you in peace. Come Anna, make your curtsey to Lord Hexham and we shall be on our way.' She turned to Donne. 'Is the carriage waiting?'

'Yes, my lady. It has been ready an hour or more,' the butler replied pointedly. He had always been an ally of Maude's.

If his new employer heard any reproach in these words, he ignored it, merely looking at Maude again as if seeing for the first time that she was dressed for travel. His gaze took in the two trunks and then settled on the little girl, who came forward and curtseyed prettily.

'Hello, uncle. I'm Anna, and you're late. It's rude to be late.'

'Anna!' Maude took hold of her daughter's hand, mortified at the child's lack of manners. 'Please excuse her, my lord, she is anxious to leave.'

'No, I am not. I want to stay here. In my room.'

'I have told you, it is no longer your room.' Maude tugged Anna towards the front door. 'And Lord Hexham is not your uncle. Now come along.'

'Wait.' Lord Hexham's voice stopped them in their tracks, and against her will, Maude turned to look at him. He was frowning even more than before, and this time his scowl was directed at her. He took a few steps towards her and spoke for her ears only, lowering his voice so that the servants would not hear. 'Why exactly are you leaving, madam? This is your home, is it not?'

'Hexham Hall belongs to you now. All of it,' Maude pointed out. Surely the solicitor must have told him that already?

'Yes, but you are family. I cannot simply cast you out.'

'Can you not? I was under the impression we would not be welcome.'

'I have no idea who told you that, but they were mistaken.'

'But surely after what happened in the past...?' Maude felt confusion swirl inside her. Why on earth would he want her under his roof? And how could he expect her to stay in the same house as a man who had not cared enough about her to find out why she did not come to meet him at the appointed hour? But perhaps he had finally understood that she had not acted of her own volition all those years ago.

'The past is just that, past,' he said, his voice

harsher than before. 'I never sought to be in this position. Indeed, I had not thought to set foot here again, but with both my uncle and cousin gone, I had no choice but to sell my commission and come back. That does not mean I wish you to leave. I shall need your guidance in matters of the estate. I was never expected to take over the running, and so no one saw fit to teach me anything about it.'

'I am sure the steward can do that. I am a mere woman, after all. That was never my domain.'

That was not quite true, as Maude well knew. The steward, Mr Aiken, was an incompetent man. He had only been kept on by Edward because Edward himself did not understand figures and so had never realised the extent of Aiken's mismanagement. Maude had tried to tell him, but to no avail.

'Much you know about it,' Edward had sneered at her. 'Stick to household matters and don't meddle in mine.'

It was no use protesting that the two went together, and that without a proper income from the estate, she could not run the household correctly.

She took a deep breath now. She wanted to grab her daughter's hand and run. Just seeing Luke again after such a long time was agony, and she realised that all the feelings she had once had for him were still there, as raw as they had been eight years previously. And as he continued to look at her coldly, she knew that this time they were not reciprocated. Perhaps never had been, except as a youthful infatuation.

'Where would you go?' he asked, glancing at the darkness and inclement weather outside.

'I... To an inn at first, and then I shall seek employment as a housekeeper. I have written to a good agency in London and they have promised to assist me.'

'Ridiculous.'

'What! How dare you?' Maude felt her cheeks turn pink with anger. What right did he have to criticise her plans? How dare he dismiss them with just that one word? 'I have to provide for my daughter somehow, since your cousin did not see fit to do so,' she replied, raising her chin a notch.

'He obviously thought I would see to it.'

Maude gave a mirthless laugh. 'I doubt he thought any such thing. He knew your views on our marriage.'

Her father-in-law had taken great pleasure in showing her a curt letter Luke had written congratulating his cousin on his marriage. 'I am sure he and his bride will deal admirably together. They are well matched in duplicity and deviousness. I am sure she will enjoy her new title to the full,' it read.

That was when Maude had realised that Luke thought she had only been toying with his feelings, and had intended to marry Edward all along. That her only ambition was a title. He could not have been more wrong.

'Nevertheless, I am not a complete cad,' he said now, his voice still low so that it would not carry, but with enough force to convince her, 'and I will provide adequately for my relations. You will please stay here for as long as you wish.'

'No. Thank you.'

He took another step closer and Maude felt her heart beat faster. His nearness was disturbing and she could not look him in the eye.

'What do you mean, no?' His scowl became even more pronounced.

'I mean, I cannot stay here with you. It would not be seemly. You … you are not married, or so I have been told.'

'You think I have designs on your virtue?' She heard the bitterness in his voice and looked up, catching a glint of something in his eyes – anger, perhaps? Then he laughed, and the sound cut through her most cruelly.

'No, but you cannot want me under your roof after … after what happened.' She was whispering, embarrassed to have to spell it out to him.

'I told you, it was a long time ago. It is no longer relevant. The welfare of my cousin's child is more important. Now, please, no more excuses. Why don't you go back to your room and prepare yourself for dinner? And the little one as well. I would like to get to know her.'

Maude took a deep breath, unsure whether to accept, but in the end the needs of her daughter took precedence over her own feelings. If Anna could stay here, she would have far better prospects as a relative of Lord Hexham than as the daughter of someone's servant.

'I will stay on – on one condition.'

'And that is?'

'That you employ me as your house-keeper. I will not remain here otherwise, an unpaid drudge and poor relation.'

'You think that is how I would treat you?'

'I have no idea, but that is what I would be in effect.'

'Isn't there a housekeeper here already? Mrs Simpkins?'

'She retired – quite some years ago now – and she was unfortunately never replaced.'

'I see.' He narrowed his eyes, as if weighing up his options, then nodded. 'Very well, but I should like you to take your meals with me unless I have company, please. You and the child. Agreed?'

'If you insist, but not tonight. Anna has had too much excitement for one day.' *And my nerves would not stand it,* Maude added silently.

'Very well.'

Maude did not like his last proviso one bit, but there was no more time to argue. Anna, who had been listening to their exchange with wide eyes, grabbed Maude's hand and shouted, 'We're staying? Hurrah!'

She turned to Donne and commanded imperiously, 'Have my trunk taken up to my room, if you please.'

'Anna, really!' Maude was once again mortified, but she knew that Donne had a soft spot for her daughter and didn't mind being ordered about by her. Indeed, he only smiled and nodded.

'Of course, Miss Anna, right away. Hardy? You heard the young lady.'

One of the footmen hurried to do the

butler's bidding and Maude soon found herself upstairs again in the guest room she had occupied since her husband's death. It had not felt right to stay in the master bedroom suite somehow, and she had been glad to escape its confines.

Anna came dancing in, her brown curls bouncing. 'See, Mama, didn't I tell you? We're family so this is our house too.'

Maude took a deep breath and prepared to try and explain to her daughter once more that they were only there on sufferance. She was not at all convinced that Luke saw them as family. More like a burden he would gladly have done without.

Looking at Anna's happy face, however, she could not disillusion her – so in the end she just murmured, 'Perhaps, dearest, perhaps.'

CHAPTER THREE

Maude was determined not to be beholden to Luke for anything, so the following morning she was up early, making sure that all was in order and the staff were performing their duties. She spoke to the butler, who told her everything was running smoothly. She then conferred with the cook about the various dishes that would be offered to his lordship for breakfast and tried to plan a menu for other meals for the week. This was rather hampered by the fact that she had no housekeeping money as yet and there was little in the larder.

'You will have to speak to the new master, my lady,' the cook grumbled. 'I am not a magician that can conjure meals out of thin air.'

'You are right, Mrs Mason. I will do so as

soon as the opportunity presents itself.'

In the event, that proved to be shortly after breakfast, when Maude was summoned to the estate office. Luke was sitting behind the desk, which was piled high with papers and ledgers that looked as though a whirlwind had gone over them. His expression was, if anything, even grimmer than the night before.

He looked up when she entered and glared at her accusingly. 'So you thought to leave me with this mess, did you? Well, let me tell you – you are not going anywhere until you have helped me sort it out. This is abominable.'

'I beg your pardon?' Maude squared her shoulders. 'What are you talking about, may I ask?'

He waved a hand to indicate the papers strewn about in front of him. 'This. The accounts. The running of the estate.'

'I told you, that is Mr Aiken's task. I was discouraged from "meddling". In fact, the solicitor specifically instructed me not to touch anything.'

'Well, you damn well should have,' Luke grumbled. 'And as for Aiken, I have just dismissed him. A more incompetent fellow I have yet to come across. What was Edward thinking, employing such a man? He could not even add up, for Heaven's sake!'

'I did tell Edward that, but he said my own mathematical skills were at fault. As long as Aiken provided him with funds on a regular basis, he did not question the man's methods.'

Luke shook his head. 'I have no idea how he did that, since there seems no rhyme or reason to these accounts. Either way, we are starting with a clean slate as of today.' He held up a brand new ledger and indicated the first page which was blank.

'We?' Maude repeated.

'Yes, we. There is no need to pretend with me, Maude, I know you were never obtuse. In fact, your brain is as sharp as mine.'

When Maude opened her mouth to protest, he held up a hand. 'No, I won't listen to any more argument. Come, take a seat here beside me and let us make a start. The sooner we sort this out, the better it will be. I need to know if this estate is producing any profit at all, and if not, why not. You should be able to help me make sense of the various entries. It has been too long since I lived here, and some of the tenants have changed. I can barely remember the names of the various farms, let alone who lives there.'

'Very well, I shall do my best. On one condition.'

He frowned at her. 'You seem to have a lot of those.'

'This one is not for myself.'

'What is it, then?'

'I will help you if you promise to pay the staff their wages immediately for the last quarter – as soon as you know whether you have the finances for it. And you will need to pay some of the tradesmen, because most of them have stopped their deliveries until further notice.'

'Damnation! Beg your pardon, but really,

what has been going on here?'

He broke off, took a deep breath and pushed his fingers through his hair. Maude noticed that it was longer than when she had last seen him, the dark brown waves brushing his collar. She suppressed a sudden longing to run her own fingers through those dark tresses and averted her gaze.

'But of course I shall be paying their wages,' he added. 'I do not expect people to work for me for nothing.'

'I am sorry you had to come back to this,' she said softly. 'I have done what I could, but Edward was away a lot and … well, he wasn't the easiest of men to deal with.'

Luke picked up an old ledger. 'The sooner we make a start, the quicker we will have some idea of how matters stand. In the meantime, I will pay the staff what they are owed, and you may send any tradesmen to me. I shall pay for victuals.' He shook his head again. 'Just as well I did not spend all the money I received when I sold out.'

'Thank you.'

He pushed the inkstand towards her. 'Probably best if you do the writing, it will be neater than mine.'

They became quite caught up in trying to unravel what Aiken had done – or not done, as proved to be the case most of the time – and they both looked up with surprise when Donne knocked on the door and came in to inform them that luncheon was served.

'Thank you, Donne. Good lord, is it really midday already?' Luke took out his pocket watch to check, as if he did not quite believe the butler.

The man nodded, but before he left, Luke noticed that he sent them a strange look and opened his mouth as if to comment on something, but then thought better of it.

Luke turned to Maude and suddenly realised that they had been sitting with their heads close together, bent over the ledgers, and that to the butler this might have seemed rather intimate. 'Dash it all,' he muttered.

Maude had busied herself with tidying

some of the piles of papers, but looked up at his words. 'What is the matter, my lord?'

Luke frowned at her use of his title. She had not always been so formal with him – but then things had changed. And not for the better.

'Did you see the expression on Donne's face?'

'What expression?' Maude blinked in confusion, and Luke almost swore out loud. Her eyes were the brilliant blue of cornflowers and he could not help but remember how they used to sparkle at the sight of him. It was no wonder he had been taken in by her.

He swallowed hard and buried the memories deeper in his mind. There was no point dwelling on them. Maude had made her choice.

He dragged his thoughts back to the present. 'Your ... er, that is to say, *my* butler seems to disapprove of us being alone together.'

'Oh. I did try to tell you yesterday, but you said...'

'We are family – yes, I know. Still, I do not suppose the local gossips will see it that way and I do not wish to add grist to their mill. You will have to have a chaperone.'

'Surely not? I am your housekeeper and a respectable widow. The house is full of servants, so there are people about all the time.'

'Won't wash.'

'But where will I find a chaperone? Besides, I doubt there is enough money to pay for one.' She indicated the books before them. 'Perhaps it is best that I leave after all.' She stood up and shook out her skirts.

'No!' He startled himself with the vehemence in his voice and made an effort to moderate his tone before adding, 'I mean, can we not just invite some female acquaintance of yours, or a relative, to stay for a while?'

Maude thought for a moment. 'There is Eliza, I suppose. She has often stayed here to keep me company while Edward was in London.'

'Eliza Manning, the vicar's daughter?' Luke

snorted. 'That whey-faced friend of yours who was forever trailing after you when you were younger? A great nuisance, she was.'

Maude frowned at him. 'There is nothing wrong with Eliza's looks. Being pale is very fashionable, I will have you know. And she never complained about having to be the third wheel when…' She caught herself, and Luke saw her take a deep breath. 'In short, she might do. She is a widow now herself, and lives nearby at Holby Manor.'

Luke stroked his chin. 'Ah, I do remember that. Old Gascombe's estate, was it not?'

'Yes. Eliza married him.'

'The devil she did! I mean, beg pardon, but … was he not in his dotage?' Luke was shocked that such a young girl should have been married off to a man more than twice her age, but Maude shrugged.

'She was not coerced, she agreed to it readily enough. He was quite rich, after all, and she had no dowry to speak of.'

Luke wanted to protest further, but thought better of it. 'Please invite her, then.

Ask her to come as soon as she can.' Maude nodded. 'Now we had better go and eat, or else Cook will be offended.'

As he held open the door for her to pass through, he suddenly recalled her daughter. 'Where is young Anna this morning? At her lessons?'

'Er, no, I have been teaching her myself – and since I have been busy with you, I expect she has been in the kitchen. Mrs Mason is very patient with her and allows her to help a little with baking and such things.'

'Should she not have a governess? How old is she?'

'Anna is six and as I had the time, it seemed easier for me to teach her myself to begin with.'

Maude would not meet his eye, and Luke suspected that was not the whole truth. He guessed there had not been money for a governess. This made him frown. What had his cousin been doing? The estate was in a mess, the house dilapidated, the servants unpaid and tradesmen refusing to bring supplies. It was all a shambles.

In Luke's uncle's day, the estate had been very prosperous and Luke did not recall any penny-pinching being necessary. So what had brought the family to these straits?

'What happened to your dowry?' he blurted, thinking out loud. They had reached the main hall by now and were about to enter the morning room where the family had always taken meals when there were no guests.

Maude threw him a startled look over her shoulder. 'M-my dowry? I do not know. I mean, it was not so large. Papa's estate was entailed to some cousin or other.'

Luke frowned. 'I shall have to have a word with the solicitor. He wrote to me, of course, but I shall need to discuss things with him in person. I noticed from the letter I received that his office is in the nearest town.'

'Yes, indeed. I'm sure he would be only too happy to come and see you.'

'Mama, there you are! And Uncle Luke – look, there is an omelette for your lunch and I helped make it.' The little whirlwind that was Anna came rushing towards them, cutting off the conversation. Luke saw Maude shake her head at her daughter.

'Lord Hexham is not your uncle. You are to address him as "my lord".'

But Luke had had enough of formality. 'Nonsense,' he said and lifted the little girl up high so that she squealed with pleasure. 'Uncle Luke sounds fine to me. If I may call you Anna?'

She giggled as he put her down. 'What else would you call me?'

'Well, I could have called you Miss Hexham, but that sounds so grand, I'd have to bow every time I said it.' He made her an exaggerated bow as if she was a queen and he her courtier. Anna laughed again.

'Silly,' she said. 'Not even Donne calls me that. But when I have my first season, all the boys will have to, won't they?'

Luke took her hand and steered her towards the table. 'Yes, unless there is one in particular that you like above the rest. Then you can allow him to call you by your pretty name. But that won't be for a while yet, now will it? So let's try this omelette of yours, shall we?'

Luke caught Maude's gaze as Anna settled in her chair. She seemed torn between horror and amusement at her daughter's high spirits, but he thought he saw relief as well.

'Thank you,' she murmured when he held out a chair for her, and sent him a small smile, the first genuine one he had seen from her since he arrived the day before. He formed the impression that she was thanking him for his patience with the child, as well as for his courtesy.

He was annoyed with himself for being pleased that he had made her happy when she had broken his heart. To distract himself from thinking about it further, he turned to Anna. At least the child was easy to talk to and he did not have to pretend with her.

'So, do you ride well, Anna?'

Maude looked up when she heard Luke ask her daughter this question. Up until that point, she had concentrated on her food and taken no part in the conversation. They had not seemed to need her to, as they were getting on famously. Maude listened with wonder, but also sadness. *If only Edward had treated his daughter the same way,* she thought.

'No, I've never learned,' Anna replied.

'You've never been on a horse?' Luke frowned at Maude, making it clear that she had been very remiss in not teaching her child such a basic skill.

'Yes, once or twice, but not on my own. Papa sold the pony.'

Luke lifted his eyebrows at Maude, as if waiting for an explanation. She cleared her throat. 'Horses are expensive, as you must know, my lord, and Edward considered it a waste to keep a pony. He, uhm, needed the money for something else at the time and never got around to replacing it.'

'It was Joseph's pony, but Papa said he'd never need it now so there was no point keeping it,' Anna put in.

'Who is Joseph?' Luke looked confused.

Maude stilled, her entire body turning to ice. How was it possible that he didn't know?

'My brother, of course,' Anna said. 'You know, the one that's in heaven now.' She had a child's simple view of things and believed wholeheartedly that her brother was now in a better place, just as Maude had told her.

Maude thought she heard Luke swear under his breath and then he turned to her, his green eyes wide with consternation. Maude swallowed hard and stared at her plate where a piece of rapidly congealing omelette no longer seemed so inviting.

'I am so sorry, I had no idea,' she heard Luke say. 'I mean, no one informed me. I assumed... Forgive me.'

Maude shook her head and attempted a smile. 'There is nothing to forgive. If no one told you, then how could you have known?'

Inside, she was seething at the fact that neither her father-in-law or Edward informed Luke of Joseph's birth or death, but it certainly was not his fault. She took a deep breath to regain her composure.

'Joseph died of congestion of the lungs when he was four. Anna was three at the time, so she barely remembers him, do you, my love?'

She had trained herself not to show any outward emotion when speaking about Joseph, since that had irritated Edward no end – even though it still cut her like a knife to even think about her little boy.

Anna shook her head. 'No, but I remember the pony.'

Luke reached out a hand and put it over Maude's, which was resting on the table. 'I am very sorry for your loss,' he said softly, and she could see that he meant it. He genuinely had not wanted to inherit the title and estate because of the death of a little boy, she was sure.

'Thank you,' she replied and pulled her hand away. His hand felt so warm and solid on top of her smaller one, but she could not bear prolonged contact. His touch had made a frisson dart through her and she did not wish to let him see that he affected her in any way. She still had her pride, even if she had nothing else left.

She pasted a smile on her face. 'Anna does not need to ride. We go for long walks in the nearby woods and that is exercise enough for a young lady, is that not so, my dear?'

'I s'pose.' Anna looked doubtful, but then her little face brightened and she smiled at Luke. 'But maybe Uncle Luke could teach me? You have a horse, don't you? I heard it last night.'

'Anna, do not badger Lord Hexham. That's most unseemly,' Maude admonished sternly.

Luke smiled back at the girl, however, and nodded. 'That's a capital idea, but I don't think old Blue is quite suitable for you. Leave it with me and I shall see if I cannot borrow a pony for you from one of our neighbours.'

'Oh, thank you!' Anna was out of her chair and had flung her arms round Luke's neck before a scandalised Maude had time to even open her mouth to protest.

Maude could not understand why her daughter was behaving so freely with Luke.

With her father, the child had been reserved and quiet. It was only with her mother and some of the servants that she chattered on in this way. And as for embracing a complete stranger – Maude really did not know what to think.

To her relief, Luke took it in good humour. 'Don't thank me yet,' he said. Then he turned to Maude again. 'What about you, Maude, do you ride these days? I seem to remember you used to be forever in the saddle.'

She felt her cheeks heat up. That was how they had always met, back when they were courting, on the pretext of riding together for exercise. Maude's groom had been amenable to bribery and often let the two of them gallop off ahead of him after Luke had slipped him a coin. Maude still remembered the excitement of those days.

'I don't have a horse either,' she admitted now. 'When Blossom died, she was never replaced.'

She didn't tell Luke that at that time, Edward had just had a particularly bad run of luck at the gaming tables and Maude had been struggling to find enough money to run the household, never mind buy a horse.

Luke's mouth tightened. 'We'll have to see about finding you a mount too, then. Leave it with me.'

'There is no need,' Maude protested. 'I am perfectly happy to walk.'

'Nevertheless, if we are to teach Anna to ride, you will need one. I cannot take the child out alone.'

Maude liked the sound of that 'we', but she refused to acknowledge it even to herself. It was only wishful thinking on her part.

CHAPTER FOUR

Eliza Gascombe arrived the very next day, and the entire household was left in no doubt as to how pleased she was to have been invited.

'My dearest Maude, what a lovely surprise it was to receive your little note. I came at once, of course. Couldn't possibly leave you in the lurch and I quite understand. Such a delicate situation, is it not?' she added in a theatrical whisper, 'and so difficult for you, isn't it?'

Maude gritted her teeth and pasted on a smile. No doubt the entire neighbourhood was gossiping about the fact that she was left with nothing, but she was determined not to let anyone know how angry and hurt she felt.

'Not at all. I have accepted the fact that this all belongs to Edward's cousin now. I am grateful that Anna and I are allowed to stay.'

'But of course he could not throw you out! That would have been most callous, and I don't remember Luke – that is to say, Lord Hexham as I suppose we must call him now – in short, he was never the heartless type.'

Maude reflected that Eliza obviously did not know about Luke's sudden departure after the fiasco of the supposed elopement, which was just as well. She had never talked to anyone about it and had no wish to discuss it now. She linked arms with Eliza and led her towards a small sitting room at the back of the house. 'Let's have some tea. I believe Cook has made muffins. I know they are your favourites.'

Maude was not convinced the servants were as happy to see Eliza as she was to be there. Donne was wearing his sternest face as he ordered their guest's trunks to be taken upstairs, and Maude saw the maids grimace at each other. Every time she stayed at Hexham Hall, Eliza was always curt to the point of rudeness with servants. Although Maude suspected it was because she herself came from a rather humble background and wanted to make sure everyone knew she was now a lady of some standing, it could make life difficult sometimes.

She sighed inwardly. Perhaps inviting Eliza had not been such a good idea, but it was too late now. She was here and she was usually good company, which was something at least.

Luke was out for most of the day, and did not meet his guest until supper time. He came down to find Eliza waiting in the salon for him. As he entered, she came towards him with her hands outstretched, as if they had been the best of friends, which was not the case at all. He reminded himself he must not forget to call her Mrs Gascombe now.

'My dear Lord Hexham, how lovely to see you again! And so kind of you to invite me. As I was telling Maude, I was of course thrilled to be of service. I will be glad to stay as long as you need me.'

He took her hands reluctantly and bowed over them, but let go as soon as he possibly could. He remembered Eliza as rather plain, with brown hair and hazel eyes, but looking at her now, he had to admit she had grown more attractive with age. He supposed she had only seemed plain to him because he had always compared her to Maude whose cool blonde beauty outshone every other lady in the county. It still did.

'I find it hard to believe that Maude is a dowager now, don't you?' Eliza laughed, a pretty tinkling sound, although rather artificial to Luke's mind. 'But then I would have been, too, if Gascombe had had any heirs. Lucky for me he did not.'

Luke frowned. 'Surely she is not a dowager until such time as I marry?'

'Perhaps not, but to all intents and purposes...'

At this moment, Maude came into the room and interrupted her friend. Anna was skipping along behind her and Maude put out a restraining hand to keep the child in check. 'Good evening, my lord. Are you sure you still want Anna to sit with us at table? She could easily have a tray upstairs.'

Her fine blue eyes seemed anxious as they passed between him and Eliza, and Luke wondered why. He had his answer soon enough.

'The child is eating with us?' Eliza sounded surprised. 'Really, Maude, I would have thought that is at least ten years too soon.'

Luke narrowed his eyes. 'It is on my orders, Mrs Gascombe. I believe it will do her good to learn how to behave in company and as there is no one here, apart from yourself, what harm can it do? She can learn from our example. Since you have come to lend Maude countenance, I quite see you as a member of the family.' He added this last sentence on purpose, and the flattery worked, just as he had thought.

'Family? Oh, yes, of course. Then naturally I can have no objections to, er ... eating with a child present.'

Eliza cast Anna a look of acute dislike, which Luke noticed was returned in full measure by a glare from the little girl. He hid a smile.

'Shall we go into the dining room, then?' He offered his arms to both ladies, and winked at Anna who brought up the rear.

'I'm sorry I only have two arms,' he told her with a smile over his shoulder. 'You do not mind being without an escort?'

She grinned at him. 'No. I couldn't reach your arms anyway, could I?'

A few days later Maude was sitting in the nursery on the top floor of the house with Anna, teaching her sums, when there was a peremptory knock on the door. To her considerable surprise, Luke entered. He smiled at Anna.

'Good morning. I am sorry to interrupt your lesson, but there is something I particularly want to show you.' He looked at Maude. 'Do you mind? It will not take long.'

She had stood up as he entered and although she was not sure what he was up to, she nodded. 'By all means.'

'You should probably come along as well,' he said, almost as an afterthought. Maude picked up her skirts and followed him down the stairs.

'Where is Mrs Gascombe this morning?' he asked along the way.

'She takes her breakfast in bed,' Maude informed him, trying not to show how much this annoyed her. Eliza may be a guest, but she was supposed to be chaperoning Maude and she could hardly do that from her bedroom. Also, Eliza had the maids running up and down the stairs because there was always something not quite right with the food they brought her. Maude had already endured a half hour of complaints from Mrs Mason on the subject.

'Good,' was all Luke said, however.

He led them out of the house, round the back into the stable yard. He nodded at one of the grooms, loitering just inside the doors of a loose box. The lad came out leading a small, sturdy pony. Anna squealed with joy.

'Is he for me? You borrowed him so I could learn?'

'Not exactly. I decided to buy him because his owner was letting him go cheaply. What do you think? Will he do?'

'Oh, Uncle Luke!' Anna was almost incoherent with joy and threw herself at him, giving his middle a fierce hug. Then she went over to the pony, approaching him almost with reverence. 'Hello, what's your name then? You're beautiful! Absolutely lovely.'

Maude, who had been almost as surprised as her daughter at this kind gesture, had to smile. The tubby pony looked as if he had been dragged through a hedge backwards and the word 'beautiful' was not one she would have used. She looked up and caught Luke's gaze on her.

'Beauty is in the eye of the beholder, is it not?' he murmured, and for some reason this made Maude's cheeks heat up as she remembered that he had once thought her beautiful.

She focused on the pony and smiled. 'Indeed. Thank you – you've made Anna very happy. It was most kind of you.'

'Nonsense. I cannot have it be said that I have mistreated my relations. Young ladies need to learn to ride. What do you say? Shall we try a short outing this afternoon with Anna on a leading rein?'

'But I don't have–' Maude started to protest, but Luke held up his hand and nodded to his left.

'Yes, you do. Go and say hello to May-flower. She's not quite as fine a horse as Blossom was, but I hope she will do? It was the best I could find at such short notice.'

Maude blinked. Another groom had led out a pretty white mare who stood tossing her head and staring at her new mistress.

'I ... thank you. She's perfect,' Maude breathed. She was astonished at his thoughtfulness, and that he even remembered her old horse's name.

Luke laughed. 'Now you are being as blind as your daughter.'

Maude walked over to the mare and made friends, stroking the soft muzzle and murmuring softly. 'Don't pay any attention to him,' she told the horse. 'He's just being rude.'

'Here, perhaps this will make amends.' Luke pulled a carrot out of his pocket and fed it to the horse. 'And I apologise if I hurt your feelings, Mayflower.' He was grinning, however, so Maude did not think he was being serious. She shook her head at him.

This was a playful side she had not thought to see in him ever again.

Anna came over and demanded to be allowed to ride that instant, so Luke lifted her onto the pony and led her round the yard a few times. 'That's enough for now,' he said. 'We're going for a proper ride after lunch.'

To Maude's surprise, Anna did not protest – and the child even remembered to thank him again before they went back to the school room.

'He is the best uncle in the world, isn't he?' she asked her mother with shining eyes as they sat down to continue the maths lesson.

Maude could only agree, but although she was grateful to him, she knew it placed her even further in his debt. How would she ever repay him?

'You are marvellously patient with the child, my lord. You could just let the groom teach her, you know. I am sure you have far more important matters to attend to.'

Eliza had of course needed to be included

on their ride, and she had been watching Luke and Anna with a deepening scowl ever since they set out. He was riding beside the girl, showing her how to hold the reins, how to position her legs and feet and how to keep her back straight. Maude agreed that he was patience personified, but wished Eliza would keep her thoughts to herself. She was sure Anna would listen much more readily to Lord Hexham than to any groom, since she seemed to like him so much.

She glanced at the man who followed them at a short distance. Luke had introduced him before the ride. 'This is Stetson. He's been with me ever since I first arrived in Portugal.' Maude had gathered that Stetson was now Luke's personal servant, but from the way they spoke to each other, they were almost like old friends. She supposed that if you had faced death together with someone, a bond was bound to develop.

Either way, Stetson did not seem to take advantage of it in any way and was a pleasant, easy-going man.

'I enjoy teaching Anna,' came Luke's calm reply to Eliza, and of course there was nothing she could say to that.

'I marvel how you all like horse-riding so much anyway,' Eliza grumbled under her breath. 'It was all you ever wanted to do when you were younger, and I could not understand it. Nasty, smelly creatures, horses.'

Maude gave a non-committal answer. If Eliza did not feel the thrill of being on the back of a horse, or want to gallop full tilt with the wind rushing past, then it was not something she could explain. All she knew was that she had always loved it, and so had Luke.

She glanced at him and in that instant he looked up and their eyes met. He smiled as if he knew what she was thinking, and he probably did. They had often been able to tell each other's thoughts when they were courting because they were so similar in many respects. They both loved being out-doors, riding recklessly, and they shared a liking for many other things as well. They had been perfect for each other.

That thought made Maude turn away abruptly. That was a long time ago and it was no longer true. She simply could not allow herself to dwell on what might have been. It was too late.

'So Stetson, have you picked up any interesting gossip below stairs?'

Luke was tying his cravat while Stetson busied himself with clearing away the shaving paraphernalia.

'Well, I have heard one or two interesting snippets, yes. Mostly they concern her ladyship.'

'You mean Maude?' Luke saw Stetson make a disapproving face. 'I know, I should not call her that, but I have known her since we were babes-in-arms.' He knew he ought not to be so familiar with her, but whenever he thought of her as Lady Hexham, it was as his cousin's wife and that still rankled. Besides, she had not forbidden him to use

59

her first name.

'Go on then, tell me what they're saying. Do they like her? Loathe her?'

'Adore her, more like.' Stetson sniffed as if he didn't hold with servants being that fond of their mistress. 'Talk about her like she is some sort of angel and won't hear a word against her.'

'Really? I would have thought that once she got the title she wanted, she would have lorded it over them.'

That was not entirely true. The Maude he had known had always been kind to servants. But then the Maude he'd known had claimed she did not want to marry his cousin either, nor cared whether she had a title or not. She had clearly lied.

He clenched his fists as he shrugged into his tight-fitting jacket, helped by Stetson. His uncle and Maude's father had always had it in mind that she should marry Luke's cousin Edward. Sir Richard Bellamy had refused to accept Luke's suit because he was not the heir of any property and had no prospects. He still remembered the humiliation he had felt when he had screwed up his courage and gone to ask for her hand. Sir Richard had merely laughed and shown him the door.

'That is not what I am hearing, or seeing for that matter,' Stetson interrupted his thoughts. 'She is always gracious and mindful of others. Her husband left her here on her own for months on end, apparently, with barely any money to run the place.' Stetson sniffed again. 'A gambling man, so I'm told.'

'Edward? I don't remember him as being that bad.' Luke frowned. Edward had not been particularly clever, but he had never been stupid enough to play too deeply when they were young. Perhaps things had changed.

Stetson coughed and cleared his throat. 'Wasn't too happy about his marriage, I gather.'

'What?' Luke found it hard to believe that anyone could be unhappy while married to

61

Maude. And Edward had wanted her, there had been no doubt about that. It had been a great source of satisfaction to him when he thought he had won her from under his cousin's nose.

'There was some talk of an elopement. His lordship was not happy about having someone else's "leftovers", as the head groom put it. You wouldn't know anything about that, my lord, would you?'

Stetson looked innocent enough, but Luke knew the man wasn't stupid and could put two and two together. He had never told him anything about Maude, but then again Stetson had not asked.

'No,' he replied curtly. 'Must have been after I left.'

'Er, quite so, my lord.'

So Edward had resented Maude for choosing Luke first and then changing her mind? It did not really make sense, but then he had always had trouble figuring out Edward's way of thinking. He sighed now.

'So Edward spent time in London gambling, did he? Is that what they are saying?'

'Yes, my lord. Although he sometimes brought friends home for weeks on end and drank the cellar dry by all accounts.'

Luke wondered what Maude thought of that – but maybe she had joined in the revelry? Either way, he was not about to ask her. He could, however, speak to the solicitor, who might know a bit more. He resolved to send for the man as soon as possible.

CHAPTER FIVE

Before Luke had time to summon anyone, however, a commotion in the hall heralded the arrival of a guest. Luke was just coming down the stairs when Donne opened the door to a young man who seemed vaguely familiar.

'Good morning,' he heard the newcomer say. 'Kindly tell his lordship that Mr

Thomas Hexham is here to see him. And have my luggage brought in. I shall be staying the night.'

Oh, shall you indeed? Luke thought, wondering what had brought his cousin to visit. A cousin he had not seen since they were both in leading strings. Then it hit him. *Of course, he is my heir! Damnation.*

He descended the stairs and held out his hand. 'Thomas, what a surprise. What brings you to these parts? I thought you still resided somewhere in deepest Yorkshire.'

Thomas bowed and shook the proffered hand somewhat limply. He was tall and thin, with fair hair and a long nose, his features pleasant, if unremarkable. 'Indeed, I do, but I felt it incumbent upon me to come and pay my respects to the new head of the family. I did as much for Edward, although you were not here at the time so of course you will not know that.'

'Er, no, I was unaware of that fact. Welcome to Hexham Hall.'

Luke glanced at Donne, who seemed to

have the situation under control.

'Perhaps you would like some refreshment?'

'Thank you, yes.'

Luke led the way to the library and the ever-efficient Donne soon appeared with a tray of wine and biscuits.

'I must say, news travels fast,' Luke commented, when they were seated on either side of the fireplace with a glass of wine. 'I have been back in England for only a couple of weeks.' He smiled at his cousin, trying to make a joke out of it, but the truth was that he was annoyed Thomas had come sniffing around so soon. He could at least have given Luke a chance to settle into his inheritance before hoping for him to shuffle off his mortal coil, he thought sourly.

Thomas did not seem amused. 'Well, a scandal such as that created by Edward spreads like wildfire, don't you know. I dare say everyone has been keeping their eyes on you ever since you set foot back in this country. I was told about it by an acquaintance recently returned from a visit to London.'

'I see. I did not realise I was the object of so much gossip.' Luke also wondered why Edward's gambling should have given rise to a scandal. It was not so unusual; many people died after accumulating gaming debts. He did not really wish to discuss it with Thomas, however, so did not comment any further.

Thomas sniffed. 'But of course. Everyone's wondering if you are going to follow in Edward's footsteps and squander the rest of the money.'

Luke gritted his teeth. No doubt Thomas was hoping for reassurance that there would be something left for him. 'I am not our cousin,' he said curtly. 'And there is nothing left to gamble with.'

Thomas's eyebrows rose. 'As bad as that, eh? Heavens.'

'Don't worry, I will sort it out, but it will take some time. Speaking of which, if you'll excuse me, I had better deal with some estate matters. I shall inform the ladies that you are

66

here and perhaps they will entertain you.'

'Ladies? I did not realise you were married.' Thomas looked surprised.

'I am not, but Edward's widow still lives here with her companion, Mrs Gascombe, and of course Edward's daughter Anna.'

'Oh, yes.'

Was it his imagination, or did Thomas look relieved? Luke wondered. As long as Luke was unmarried, there was no chance of another heir. Thomas must surely realise that Luke had plenty of time to find himself a wife, however, since he was only in his late twenties.

'I look forward to seeing you at dinner,' he said, and stalked out of the room, thinking the complete opposite.

Damned impudence!

The following afternoon Maude was in the estate office with Luke when Eliza came and knocked on the door.

'There you are! I have been looking all over the house for you. It's too bad of you, really it is. I'd be shirking my duties if I did not tell you that this simply won't do, you know.'

Maude and Luke had been bent over an old ledger with their heads close together. Aiken's scrawl was particularly bad in this one and almost impossible to decipher. They looked up as Eliza entered through the door, which they'd left open on purpose. She wagged a finger playfully at them.

'I know, I know, it's just business. I realise that – but not everyone would believe it, mark my words.'

'I am sorry, Eliza, I have only been here two minutes.' Maude straightened up and tried not to look flustered. 'I was in the garden earlier, speaking to Howson about the flowers you wanted for the arrangements.'

Eliza had taken it upon herself to put together extravagant flower arrangements for all the main rooms, and although she did undoubtedly have a knack for it, her demands had annoyed the head gardener. Maude had had to soothe his ruffled feathers and assure him that the flowers he produced were as wonderful as always.

'Yes, well, come along now. Tea is ready and Mr Hexham is waiting for us in the salon. I believe the child has helped to make some scones, too.'

Maude bit back a protest at the way Eliza always referred to Anna as 'the child' and never by her name. It was as if the little girl was not a person because she was so young, just something to be endured. It irritated Maude no end, but she supposed that if one had never had children of one's own, perhaps one saw things differently.

Her thoughts went to Luke – he had no trouble interacting with Anna. And as far as Maude knew, he had no children of his own. She shook her head and prepared to follow Eliza.

'Will you join us, my lord?' she remembered to ask just before she left.

Luke took a moment to consider this, then nodded. 'Yes, why not? I could never resist scones.'

Luke watched the two ladies as they went through the ritual of pouring the tea and offering scones around. They seemed to divide the tasks up between them without even thinking about it, with Maude filling the cups, Eliza adding milk and sugar as required and little Anna carefully carrying the plate of scones around to each person.

'Let me help you with that, Mrs Gascombe,' Thomas offered politely and took the sugar bowl from Eliza. 'You only have one pair of hands, after all.'

Eliza smiled at him, looking a trifle flushed. 'How very kind.'

Anna offered Luke the plate of scones and he took two. 'Thank you,' he said. 'Did you really help make these?'

Anna beamed with pride. 'Yes, and Cook says I have a very light hand.'

Luke had no idea what that meant, but gathered it was good, so he smiled at her. 'Excellent. Your future husband will be pleased.'

Maude looked up, but when she saw that he was joking, she relaxed. Luke wondered why she was constantly nervous about the child's behaviour when Anna seemed very well-mannered to him. Apart from her tendency to impulsive hugs, which he did not mind in the slightest, she was very biddable and only spoke out of turn occasionally.

Maude took a sip of tea, then looked at it with a frown. 'I say, this sugar is not dissolving very well. I shall have to speak to Cook and make sure it is fresh. Perhaps she used the old sugar cone? It was the same yesterday.'

'Mine is fine,' Luke commented, staring into his cup.

'And mine, Maude dear. You must be imagining it,' Eliza chimed in. 'But it is such a bore when one's servants do not listen, though, do you not think? I am forever having to remind my cook about things because she simply doesn't pay attention.'

Eliza then changed the subject, the way she always did whenever a discussion bored her, and began to gossip about their nearest neighbours. Luke thought no more about it until later that afternoon when Stetson reported that Lady Hexham had taken to her bed with a bad case of food poisoning. He supposed she must have been right, and the sugar was too old. He hoped she had remembered to ask the cook to buy a new supply.

Maude groaned and tried to make herself more comfortable. She had been suffering from severe nausea and loose bowels for an hour or more now and it seemed relentless.

'Can I get you anything?' Eliza bustled in. 'Some tea, perhaps?'

'No! No, thank you.' Maude almost groaned out loud again. 'I think it was that old sugar that did for me in the first place. Honestly, I could not face another cup today. I ... I just need to rest.'

'Very well, I shall leave you to it then. Oh, and just so that you know, Lord Hexham is taking the child riding and I thought I had better go along, just to be on the safe side.'

'Very well. Thank you. Is Cousin Thomas going with you?'

'No, he said he had had enough of riding for a while, having travelled for days to get here. Just as well. He's not exactly scintillating company, is he?' Eliza laughed.

Maude had to admit she was right. Cousin Thomas, while polite enough, did have a tendency to bore on about subjects such as farming, which did not interest the ladies at all.

Maude frowned as the door closed. She was sure Anna would have been perfectly safe with just Luke and Stetson, but she was too tired to argue. She refused to acknowledge even to herself that the thought of Eliza and Luke riding together bothered her. There was no reason why it should.

Luke had not bargained on bringing Eliza along for the riding lesson with Anna, but for once, she proved to be excellent company. She did not complain about her horse once, and kept regaling him with stories of some of the stupid things his neighbours had done while he had been away. He found her amusing and witty, if a tad sarcastic.

In the autumn sunshine, her hazel eyes sparkled and their emerald flecks were more noticeable. Her pale complexion did not seem so insipid either, especially with a becoming flush on each cheek from the exercise. Luke found himself enjoying her company for the first time.

'How long have you been a widow, if I might ask?' he said.

'Just over a year now,' she replied. Then she turned to him, her eyes wide. 'I won't pretend with you, my lord, for I feel we are old friends. I have not mourned my late husband unduly. Ours was a marriage of convenience, at least on my part; we both got what we wanted from it, no more, no less. I am sorry if that sounds callous, but it is the way of the world, is it not?'

Luke nodded. Eliza was not the first girl to marry an older man in order to gain a fortune and position in society, so how could he blame her? He had guessed from Maude's remarks that Eliza must have been left well provided for, which was as it should be. It would have been a shame if her sacrifice had been for nothing.

He smiled at her. 'But now you are free to choose another more suitable companion for yourself.' It wasn't until the words were out of his mouth that he realised it sounded as though he was flirting with her.

She sent him a coy glance, confirming that she had noticed this. 'Indeed, my lord,' she said. 'That is my intention.' She lowered her voice. 'Between you and me, what I should really like is to be as in love as Maude was.' She sent him an apologetic glance. 'I remember she was smitten with you at first, but I believe your cousin turned out to be the love of her life. She was simply devastated when he died. Such bad luck.'

Luke felt as if someone had rammed him with a knife, but he kept his expression neutral. 'I see. And was it reciprocated, this love?'

Eliza laughed. 'Hardly, especially considering how he died.'

'And how exactly was that? No one seems

to want to enlighten me.' He had asked the solicitor, but the man had muttered something unintelligible which sounded like 'some things are best forgotten'.

'I'm sorry, but that is not for me to tell you. It may only be rumours in any case, and I should hate to be the one to spread gossip.'

Well, that is a first, Luke wanted to say, but swallowed the words and suppressed a frown. Eliza gossiped entirely too much, in his opinion, but if she wanted to play games, he would not give her the satisfaction of seeing he was rattled. He abruptly changed the subject, pretending that Anna was doing something wrong so that he could ride up and show her how to do it correctly, but he could not get Eliza's words out of his mind.

Perhaps he ought to be practical himself, and marry her for convenience. He could not deny that finding a rich wife would be far easier than trying to sort out the mess his cousin had left. Having wrestled with the ledgers for nearly a week now, he had concluded that it would take a deal of work in order to return the estate to its previous prosperity. Edward had bled it dry.

He could not help but wonder, however, what had driven Edward to such excesses. The solicitor had confirmed there had been huge gambling debts to settle, and these seemed like the acts of a very reckless man. So why had he not been happy with his beautiful wife if she adored him as much as Eliza hinted? Even if they had lost their son, surely with time, they could have had other children apart from Anna?

It was a mystery, and one he was not going to solve this afternoon.

CHAPTER SIX

By Sunday, Maude had recovered suffi-ciently to go to church with everyone else. Luke and Thomas escorted the two ladies and Anna, both gentlemen deciding to ride, rather than travel in the carriage. Luke did not know why, but since the ride with Eliza he had been loath to spend much time in her company. At least not until he had decided whether or not he should court her.

'My lord, how very agreeable to welcome you back to the parish.' The vicar, a Mr Smedley who was a large, jovial man in his middle years, stood by the entrance to the little church. He shook hands with Luke. 'I do hope you have not found your new tasks too onerous. But then I am sure Lady Hexham has given you every assistance. Such a kind lady. If only…' Mr Smedley broke off abruptly. 'But we mustn't dwell on sad things. She seems happy enough now.'

'Yes, she has recovered from her grief remarkably quickly,' Luke could not help saying. Come to think of it, he could not recall Maude saying a single thing about mourning Edward. If she had been as much in love as Eliza claimed, he could only conclude that she was a very fickle woman indeed – as indicated by his own involvement with her.

Mr Smedley, however, looked startled at his words and blinked at Luke. 'Surely that is understandable in the circumstances?'

'And which circumstances would those be?'

'Well, I mean ... the way your cousin died and ... in short, I'm not surprised that...' The vicar coughed and glanced around furtively, as if making sure no one was within earshot. 'What I mean to say is, naturally it is none of my business. I am only glad to see Lady Hexham looking much more like her normal, cheerful self. And now, if you'll excuse me, my lord, I must go and prepare for the service.'

Luke was left feeling yet again as though he was missing a piece of the puzzle. As soon as he could, he would ask Stetson to find out for him. Servants always knew more than they should and he would bet his last penny they would be able to tell him how his cousin died. He should have asked them first.

'What a disagreeable, scowling man he is sometimes, to be sure.' Eliza glanced at

Luke and whispered in Maude's ear. 'It's just as well you have me to act as a buffer between you or else he might kill you with one of those dagger looks of his.'

Maude resisted the urge to stare at Luke. She had no idea what had made him cross this time, but Eliza was right – he did spend a lot of his time acting like a bear with a sore head. She only wished she knew why. It probably did not help that he was having to sort out the shambles that was now his inheritance, but she could not help but feel that her own presence contributed to his black moods.

Why, then, had he told her to stay?

She resolved to ask him again whether he would prefer her and Anna to leave. It might be the best thing all round. Upon their return to the house, however, she forgot all such thoughts when she was once again struck down with nausea and stomach cramps after lunch. She retired to her room and stayed there, being nursed by Eliza, for the next three days.

She could not travel anywhere, whether she wanted to or not.

'He did what? You must be joking.'

Luke stared at Stetson in disbelief, but the man held his ground. 'Certainly not, my lord. I have it from the butler himself, and I doubt Mr Donne has ever lied in his life. Your cousin was killed in a duel, fighting over another man's wife. It is the truth, and no mistake.'

'But that would mean...'

'He did not want his own wife, yes. I told you, my lord, he upped and left her here for months on end. Wasn't a happy marriage, so I hear.'

Luke shook his head. 'I find that strange. My cousin wanted Maude – that is, Lady Hexham – from the moment he returned from Cambridge and found that she'd turned into a beauty. He pursued her relentlessly and although she refused him initially, I have heard recently that she came to love him deeply. So why would he not have been satisfied with that?'

Stetson shrugged. 'Like I said, 'parently he didn't like taking someone else's leavings. Pr'aps he thought she wasn't, er … pure, like?'

'Nonsense. Of course she was. Maude is a lady through and through.'

And I should know, he thought to himself. But was that what Edward had believed? That Luke had seduced Maude even before their supposed elopement? It would make sense, but it still was not a very good reason for treating her so badly – and it was untrue.

'I take it my cousin lost this duel?' he asked curtly.

'In a way, although the other man died of his wounds as well. It would appear the scandal was hushed up since your cousin's opponent was someone high up in government circles.'

'Dear Lord.' Luke sighed and gritted his teeth. 'Well, thank you for letting me know. I shall have to find out more.'

Stetson was just about to leave, but turned

and asked, 'Did you know that Lady Hexham is ill again, my lord? Second time this week she's had food poisoning, although why she is the only one who keeps eating bad things, I am sure I don't know. She is one unlucky lady, I'd say.'

Luke narrowed his eyes at the man. 'The only one, you say? Yes, very strange, to be sure. I think I had better go and speak to the cook. If she is serving Lady Hexham something different to the rest of us, it will have to stop. Thank you.'

'My lord? May I have a word, please?'

Luke looked up from the papers on his desk and focused on Donne, who had presumably knocked, although he hadn't heard him. 'Oh, yes, enter.'

'It's about the rats, my lord.'

'Rats? What rats?'

'Well, there was an infestation in the cellars not long ago and although I had the ratter in, afterwards I decided I'd put out some poison, just in case. Only I have nearly run out and I wondered whether you'd allow me to order some more.'

'Yes, of course, no need to ask. I told Lady Hexham to just have all household bills sent to me.'

'I am aware of that, my lord, just thought I should check. Arsenic is a bit expensive, as you probably know.'

'Arsenic?' Luke blinked, a terrible suspicion entering his mind like a flash of lighting. 'Remind me, Donne, what does it look like?'

The butler seemed perplexed by this question, but answered all the same. 'Ah – white, a bit like sugar or salt, I should say. Why?'

'Oh, nothing.' Luke clenched his fists under the table. 'However, I do not like the thought of such poison being readily available here, so would you mind keeping it under lock and key, please? Preferably in a secret location.'

'Certainly, my lord. I shall see to it right away.'

'Excellent, thank you. Oh, and one other

thing, Donne.'

'Yes, my lord?'

'Please ask the cook to throw out all the sugar in her cupboards. It did not taste right and I would rather pay for a new cone. Wouldn't want anyone else to go down with food poisoning. I was going to tell her myself, but I have not had the time.'

Donne narrowed his eyes and nodded. 'Indeed, my lord.

Luke continued to allow Anna to eat dinner with the adults, even though Cousin Thomas did not seem to approve of this any more than Eliza did. Luke had even decreed that they would dine earlier, to suit Anna's tender years better, which Maude thought very considerate. The little girl had eagle eyes, however, and never hesitated to voice her thoughts.

'Is there something wrong with Mr Hexham's neck, Mama?' Anna whispered as she followed Maude and Eliza to the drawing room to await the two men that evening. 'It seems a bit stiff.'

Maude stifled a gurgle of laughter and tried to keep a straight face. 'No, dearest. I would hazard a guess that he is just not used to dining in the company of six-year-olds.'

Thomas had in fact spent a large portion of every mealtime gazing down his long nose at Anna, who was seated opposite him at the table. Maude had been afraid his eyes might pop out of his head the first time Luke had announced that Anna was eating with them, and Thomas did not seem to have become used to it yet. He regarded the child as if she were some sort of curiosity, to be studied and catalogued. Fortunately, his good manners prevented him from arguing with his host, however much he might wish to. And Maude had a feeling he wished to very much.

Luke never lingered long over the port and Maude happened to be standing by the door as he came in, alone. She raised her eyebrows at him. 'Where is Cousin Thomas this evening?'

Luke shrugged. 'Said he had had a long

day and begged to be excused so he could retire early.' He added with a wry grin, 'Perhaps the thought of having to spend the rest of the evening talking to Anna had something to do with it. I told him she would be joining us in a game of cards.'

Maude shook her head at him. 'Really, my lord, that was too bad of you. And you should not have insisted on her presence again. You did say she was only to eat with us if we did not have guests. Poor Mr Hexham – it is obviously not what he is used to, and you have inflicted her on him every night so far.'

'Well, he is family so I do not consider him a guest. Besides, he came uninvited and therefore I have no sympathy. Anna stays.'

The little girl must have heard her name, because she looked up and smiled at him. 'Are we playing cards, Uncle Luke?'

'Indeed we are. Your turn to deal.'

He was teaching Anna simple card games most evenings and Maude was very grateful for his attention to her daughter. It amazed her that he was not out socialising with their neighbours instead, but so far he had shown no inclination to accept any of the invitations that had come flooding in when he arrived. It was strange, but she for one, was not complaining.

If only she could have such an easy relationship with him herself – but that was impossible. She sighed and tried to concentrate on her book.

'Maude, do you have a moment, please?' Luke managed to accost her as she came down the stairs before breakfast.

She looked up in surprise, her lovely eyes like forget-me-nots covered in shining dew, but then she frowned. 'Of course. Is something the matter?'

'No, I just need to ask you something,' he said and added in a whisper, 'In private.' He nodded meaningfully towards the breakfast room, where Cousin Thomas could be heard arguing over some trifling matter with Eliza. The two hardly ever saw eye to eye, which was unfortunate to say the least. Thomas had told Luke he considered Eliza a 'fribble' with not a serious thought in her head. He had also dared to comment on her ill-treatment of a maidservant, although Eliza disputed that vehemently and said the girl had deserved being shouted at.

Luke agreed with Thomas for the most part, but he didn't see why it should irk the man so. He did not have to live with her.

Luke led the way into the library and closed the door. 'I am sorry to drag you away, Maude, but I did not want either of our guests to hear me. I merely wanted to know … how are you feeling?'

'Who, me? I am fine. Thank you.'

Luke studied her face, which although pale, seemed healthy enough. In fact, she was as beautiful as ever and the only change he saw was in her manner, which was far more serious than he remembered from years before. 'No more nausea?' he asked.

'No, not since that bout that started after church last Sunday.'

'I thought so.' It had been that day when he had had Donne lock up the rat poison. The thought made him clench his fists behind his back. He had not wished to be right in his suspicions.

'What do you mean?' Maude blinked at him, clearly alarmed now, and he hastened to reassure her.

'Nothing – I just mean that it is good you are better.'

'Yes, well I had words with Cook and she is being extra careful when preparing food now, so hopefully we should all be fine. Was that all?'

Luke noticed that Maude seemed on edge, almost as if she could not wait to get away from his company. That made him annoyed, but he did not know why he should expect anything else, after all. She had not wanted his company eight years ago, so why should she have changed her mind now?

'No,' he said curtly, then changed his mind. 'Actually, yes. Is there anything we can do to get Thomas out of the house for a while? The fellow's been here for over a week now and shows no signs of leaving. He's been hanging around the estate office, pretending he wants to help, but I suspect he is just snooping. It's damned irritating, if you'll pardon my language.'

Maude raised her eyebrows and a hint of a smile crept into her eyes, making them sparkle again. Luke wished for the umpteenth time that they were not such fine eyes, the kind a man could drown in. It made it much more difficult to maintain his anger with her for what she had done to him.

'You think he is trying to see whether there is anything left for him to inherit?' Maude asked.

'Of course. Why else would he be here? Although I will do everything in my power to make sure he is not my heir.'

'Quite,' she murmured. 'Well, the weather has been lovely these last few days. We could always arrange a picnic or some such outing and invite a few of our neighbours. You will need to meet them if you are to find a wife.

And if Mr Hexham sees you paying court to the young ladies, perhaps he will take the hint and leave?'

'I doubt it – he has not taken any so far,' Luke muttered. 'But it is an idea, to be sure. How soon can you arrange it?'

'If I ask Eliza to help me, we might be able to go this afternoon. It's a perfect day for it, after all, and I doubt anyone is all that busy at the moment. Leave it to me.'

'Thank you. I appreciate your help.'

She fled the room, like a deer running from a hunter, and he leaned his head against the cool wood of the door frame. He had to stop thinking about the past and concentrate on the future. This afternoon, he would meet some of the young ladies of the neighbourhood and he sincerely hoped there was a diamond of the first water among them. She would have to be out-standing, in order to catch his interest, because he'd never yet come across anyone who equalled Maude and he was beginning to think he never would.

Despite her treachery, she was the only woman he had ever truly wanted. She still was.

But it was clear to him that she did not love him.

CHAPTER SEVEN

With Eliza's help, Maude had a picnic organised in hours. As she had guessed, all their neighbours were as bored as they were and jumped at the chance of some socialising. They were also curious about the new Lord Hexham, and not a single one turned down the invitation to join their little cavalcade. It helped that it was a glorious autumn day, almost as warm as late summer.

'What a good idea, my lord,' Maude heard the squire's wife saying to Luke. 'We have not been to Hope Spring for ages. Now, have you met my daughter Catherine? She has been hoping to make your acquaintance ever since you returned.'

'Mama!' Catherine was just about to have her first season and blushed a lot, Maude noticed. The girl was pretty enough, with big brown eyes and chestnut curls, but next to Luke she looked impossibly young.

But perhaps that was what he would be wanting in a wife – someone young and malleable? The thought made her heart contract painfully. She felt jealousy cut through her like a vicious knife, but she had no right to feel that way. What he did was his business.

She really did not wish him to marry yet, though, she admitted to herself. She would be unable to endure watching Luke and his new wife making doe-eyes at each other. Besides, she would find it hard to relinquish the reins of running the household to some chit barely out of the schoolroom. If she stayed on as Luke's housekeeper, she would have to take orders from his future wife, which would be impossible. No, she'd have to leave.

He had to marry in order to beget an heir. She knew that. If only Joseph had lived... But she would not think about that now.

They set off in open carriages, with everyone chatting and laughing. Even Cousin Thomas joined in and was seen to smile occasionally.

Hope Spring was only an hour away, and the servants soon had rugs spread out and a meal organised. To Maude's relief, due to the short notice everyone had agreed to bring their own food, which saved her from having to explain the straitened circumstances at Hexham Hall.

'I say, he's a nice-looking young man, is he not?' The squire's wife, Lady Sutton, plumped down beside Maude and nodded in Luke's direction. Maude followed her gaze and saw Luke surrounded by young ladies, all hanging on his every word. He looked to be enjoying himself enormously, although he was kindly including Thomas in the conversation since he was sitting nearby.

'Yes, indeed,' she replied. What else could

she say, after all? There was no man in the world as handsome as Luke, in Maude's opinion, but of course she could not tell Lady Sutton that. 'He is much like my late husband in that respect,' she added, just in case the woman had thought to make any snide comments about the past. And it was true. Edward had been handsome too, although he never equalled his cousin.

'Hmph. Well, I'm glad to see he is not high in the instep. You never know what inheriting a title can do to a man. Some of them become insufferable.'

Maude smiled. 'Oh, you need have no fears on that score.'

At that moment, Anna came hurtling over and threw herself at Luke. He managed to catch her without overbalancing, and lifted her high into the air. Maude almost thought that he looked relieved to see her, but that couldn't be right. The child had interrupted his conversation with three lovely young women, and most men would have been annoyed. She was very grateful that he was not – or, at least, that he refrained from saying so.

'He seems to get on well with your little girl,' Lady Sutton commented.

'Yes, he is very patient with her. He has been teaching her to ride and bought a pony for that purpose. That was extremely kind of him.'

Lady Sutton threw her a glance which Maude couldn't quite interpret. 'Did he now? Yes, most generous of him, to be sure.'

Another lady joined them on the rug – Lady Wallace, the wife of the only other titled gentleman in the neighbourhood. She was some years older than Maude, but they had always got on very well.

'Maude, this was a wonderful idea. I was just saying to Henry yesterday that if I did not get out of the house soon, I would go completely mad.'

Maude smiled. 'Well, you could always come and visit us, you know.'

'Well, yes, but...' Lady Wallace lowered her voice. 'One doesn't like to impose, and the new Lord Hexham has not called on Henry yet, so we were not sure whether you were receiving anyone.'

'He has been rather occupied with trying to sort out estate matters,' Maude explained. 'It is all new to him, since he never expected to inherit, you know. A great deal to learn.'

'Of course, of course. Henry said to give him time. But what do you think? I really want to give a ball. Would you all come if I were to organise it for next week? Oh – and you, too, of course, Lady Sutton.'

'I cannot answer for his lordship,' Maude said, 'but you may certainly ask. Perhaps now that he has met you all again, he will be eager to venture out more.' She did not add that, for herself, she could not possibly go. It would be easier to decline in writing.

Lady Wallace beamed. 'Then I shall. We have not had a ball in ages – it will be such fun. I shall send out the invitations as soon as possible.'

It was a tired but happy group that made

their way home after the picnic. Eliza had elected to travel back with Lady Sutton, since they were in the middle of a very important conversation, which left only Maude and Anna in the open carriage. Luke and Thomas rode next to them, with Thomas actually smiling.

'Thank you for organising such an enjoyable outing, Lady Hexham,' he said to Maude. 'I have little opportunity to socialise at home.'

'Oh, and why is that?'

'Well, I live with my mother and she hardly ever goes out these days.' A shadow crossed his features. 'She does not like me to leave her side too often – it makes her nervous when I am not around. So, of course, it is my duty to stay with her.'

Maude was surprised at his words and felt very sorry for him. He was obviously a young man who took his fillial duties very seriously.

'She must be very worried by your current absence.'

'Indeed, but she knew it was only right

and proper that I should pay my respects to the new head of the family. I arranged for a friend of hers to stay with her until such time as I return.'

He seemed so sincere, Maude almost felt ashamed for suspecting him of only visiting in order to see what his future inheritance might be. She was also sorry she had not asked him about his circumstances before. She was just about to question him further, when suddenly one of the carriage horses neighed loudly and took off as if all the hounds of hell were after it. The second one had no choice but to follow and despite the coachman's best efforts, both horses bolted.

The Hexham carriage had been in the lead, so unfortunately there was no one in front to impede their progress. Anna screamed and Maude put one arm around her daughter, while holding onto the side of the carriage with her other hand. She was frozen by fear, staring at the roadside rushing by them at an alarming speed while they were being bounced around in their seat. At one point, a wheel hit a large stone and the carriage made a creaking noise as it landed again.

Maude swallowed hard and began to pray. *Please, dear God, don't let anything happen to Anna. Please, save her!*

She tried to shield Anna with her own body, in case there should be a crash, and at first she barely the voice that called out to her. 'Maude. Maude! Hand her to me. Now!'

She looked up and realised Luke was galloping alongside the carriage, endangering his own life since he was perilously close to the bushes. He stretched out one arm, however, and she understood immediately what he was trying to do. She looked into his eyes and knew that she trusted him. Without hesitation, she lifted Anna and pushed her towards him.

He put his arm around the little girl's waist and managed to scoop her up and onto the horse in front of him. 'Hold on!' he called out to Maude, before slowing down. Maude turned her head to see him hand Anna safely to Thomas before setting off after the carriage once more. She breathed a sigh of relief. At least Anna was unhurt, and perhaps soon he would manage to halt the runaway horses as well. In the next instant, however, she heard the coachman cry out and then the carriage hit a bump. There was sickening crunch, the carriage slewed sideways and was dragged along the ditch for a few yards, before hitting something solid.

Maude tried to hold on, but was conscious of sailing through the air before landing hard. Then the world went black.

'Maude? Maude, can you hear me?'

Maude heard someone groan and realised belatedly that the noise was coming from her own throat. She felt a cold hand on her brow and her eyelids fluttered open.

'What happened?' she croaked. Her mouth seemed to be filled with dust and she had trouble getting the words out.

'You have been in an accident and hit your head, but you will be fine. Just stay still, we shall soon have you home.' Luke's voice was soothing, as if he was talking to a small child, and Maude allowed herself to be reassured. She remembered he had saved Anna, so there was nothing to worry about.

'But the coachman? And the horses?' she whispered, recalling their terrified whinnying.

'They are all fine. The coachman is unhurt and calming the horses now. There is barely a scratch on them because the carriage broke loose.'

'Oh, good.' Maude closed her eyes again.

She felt herself being lifted and placed on something soft, then heard Lady Sutton giving orders. 'Place the cushion there. No, not like that, here! That's better. Do not worry, Lady Hexham, we will drive slowly to spare your poor head the jolting. And keep your wrist still. It appears a trifle swollen.'

Maude must have dozed off, because it seemed no time at all before Lady Sutton's carriage was stopping before the front door of Hexham Hall. As Maude opened her eyes, the first thing she saw was Anna sitting in the saddle in front of Luke. The little girl's eyes were huge and it was clear that she had suffered a fright, but Luke had one arm firmly around her waist and when he whispered something in her ear, she managed a smile.

Donne and the other servants came rushing out to help, but it was Luke who picked Maude up and carried her indoors. Eliza followed, with Thomas and Anna trailing behind.

'I am sure I could walk,' Maude protested feebly, Luke's nearness making her feel even weaker than the effect of her injuries alone. She could smell the clean scent of him, and heady memories of being held close to him long ago came rushing back, almost choking her in their intensity.

'Nonsense,' he replied. 'I am fairly sure you will not be going anywhere for at least a few days. I'd bet my last groat that you are suffering from concussion and your wrist is not looking good either. Sprained, no doubt.'

This turned out to be the case and Maude was ordered to stay in bed to rest. A doctor came to bandage her head and her arm, and told her sternly to stay put or he 'would not be responsible for the consequences'.

'I seem to be spending an inordinate amount of time in my room at the moment,' she complained to Eliza, who again took it upon herself to look after Maude. 'I am not much use as a housekeeper, am I?'

'It is hardly your fault,' Eliza answered. 'I am sure his lordship will not hold it against you.'

There was a waspish tone to Eliza's voice which Maude did not quite understand, but she was too tired to think about it. She just wanted to sleep.

'Should you be up and about already?' Luke frowned at Maude as she entered the breakfast room a few days after the accident. Her face was pale as newly fallen snow and there were dark smudges under her eyes, but she looked if possible even more beautiful. He gritted his teeth and tried to ignore the bolt of longing that shot through him.

'Yes, the doctor says I am fine now, thank you,' she replied. 'My wrist is still sore, but as it is the left one, it doesn't matter much.'

She helped herself to some breakfast, but Luke noticed that she ate little. Anna, on the other hand, was wolfing down toast and bacon as if there was no tomorrow.

'Whoa, whoa, slow down, young lady,' he said to her. 'What's the rush? Is the house on fire?'

'Jeffries said there are kittens in the stable and I could come and see them after break-fast. Cook is coming too because she's going to choose a new one for the kitchen. Too many mice in the pantry.'

Luke smiled. 'Well, I'm sure they'll still be there even if you take two extra minutes to chew your food.'

Eliza entered the room with Thomas and just as they sat down, Donne brought the day's mail. Luke opened his in desultory fashion, ignoring several invitations to din-ners and soirees. Despite having met the neighbours now, he had little inclination to socialise. When he came to the last one, however, he paused and read it through again.

'It would seem we are all invited to a ball at Sir Henry and Lady Wallace's,' he said without much enthusiasm. 'If I am deciphering this scrawl correctly, Lady Wallace seems to think that we have already agreed to come. Is that so?' He looked at Maude, who frowned.

'Well, I would not go so far, but she did mention it at the picnic. I only remember saying it was a nice idea.' She glanced at Luke. 'You can always decline, my lord, although the Wallaces are famous for their balls. Invitations are much sought after.'

'Then we must all go, I suppose.'

'Oh, wonderful!' Eliza smiled. 'I shall be able to wear my new rose-coloured taffeta.'

'Thomas, will you come?' Luke asked.

'Yes, of course, it will be my pleasure.'

'You will have to excuse me, I am afraid,' Maude put in. 'I really do not think it is the done thing to invite someone's housekeeper.'

She stood up, abandoning her breakfast half-eaten. 'I had better see to some of my duties.' Luke opened his mouth to protest, but she was gone before he could utter a word.

He scowled and fixed Eliza with a glare. 'That's ridiculous. You must persuade her to come, Mrs Gascombe. She went to the picnic after all, despite being in my employment.'

Eliza shrugged. 'I doubt I can sway her. Besides, it is a convenient excuse, is it not?'

'What do you mean?'

'She has nothing suitable to wear for such an occasion. Maude has not had any new clothes in years. In fact, I cannot recall the last time she attended a party of any kind.'

Eliza said this as if it was common knowledge, which annoyed Luke. He had not noticed what Maude wore, because he was usually too busy looking at her lovely face.

'That cannot be true, surely. You ladies are forever buying things or altering old gowns.'

'That just shows how much gentlemen notice.' Eliza shook her head mockingly. 'Maude has already done the best she can.

Trust me, there will not be anything worth altering in her wardrobe.'

'We'll see about that,' Luke muttered. He had a feeling this was just another excuse not to spend time in his company, and it annoyed him no end. She would not get away with it, because he was determined she was going to this ball. At least then he would be able to ask her to dance – so that he could legitimately hold her in his arms again. Even if it was only for a short while.

CHAPTER EIGHT

The knock on Maude's bedroom door was peremptory and she hurried to open it. When she found Luke outside, however, she frowned.

'My lord? Is there something wrong?' A thought struck her. 'It's not Anna, is it? Is she hurt?'

'No, everything is fine and as far as I know, nothing has happened to Anna.' To Maude's surprise, Luke swept past her and headed across her room to the wardrobe. Before she had time to protest at this intrusion, he flung open both doors and started to riffle through the contents.

'My lord, do you mind? You cannot barge in here and go through my possessions like that. What are you looking for?'

'A dress.'

'I beg your pardon?' Maude was seriously confused now and was beginning to wonder if Luke had lost his senses. 'What would you need a dress for?'

'You.' Luke completed his evaluation of her clothes and turned to look at her. 'So Eliza was right. You really don't have anything to wear.'

'What nonsense is this? I have plenty of clothes, thank you very much. Or are you saying that you find fault with the way I dress?' Maude put her hands on her hips, becoming angry now. She had no idea what had got into him and he was not making sense.

'Not in general, no – but I want you to come to the Wallaces' ball with us and I can see that there is nothing here that could be made to serve as a ball gown.'

'I told you, I have no wish to go…'

'Whether you are acting as my house-keeper or not, you are still Lady Hexham, and as such, you have every right to attend. How would it look if I was seen to exclude you? People would think it was deuced odd – and just imagine the gossip that would give rise to.'

'Well, I … had not thought of that.'

'No, I wager you had not.' He strode to-wards the door. 'This afternoon we shall go into the nearest town. There must be a seamstress there capable of making a gown quickly. If we set off directly after lunch, we should have plenty of time, and Anna can come for the ride. She would like that, wouldn't she?'

'Yes, of course, but I really don't want to be beholden to you for a gown. We shall have to go to the pawn shop first.'

'Pawn shop? Whatever for?'

'So that I can exchange my mother's diamonds for some money.'

'Absolutely not! Wear them.'

With that order and without waiting for her reply, he left the room and Maude could only stare after him.

Now what was she to do?

Luke had been appalled to find that Eliza was right about Maude's wardrobe. Although he had examined everything in there, he found nothing that was not old-fashioned, made over or plain worn out. It would seem that Edward had thought of no one but himself, spending even his wife's allowance – if she had had one, which Luke was beginning to doubt – on gambling. It angered him greatly.

He was therefore determined to make up for his cousin's shabby treatment and when he ushered Maude and Anna into a dressmaker's shop, he told the woman in no uncertain terms that he expected to be shown only the best she had to offer. Maude attempted to protest, but he shook his head at her.

'I will not have it said that I am mean to my relations,' he stated firmly, and she could not argue with that.

As well as a ball gown in shimmering mauve watered silk, he ordered several new day dresses for Maude and three for little Anna. He allowed them to choose the colours for themselves, but steered them away from the cheaper materials Maude tried to insist on.

'That is false economy and you know it,' he said. 'Especially when it comes to children.'

'Yes, but I cannot hope to repay you for any of this unless…'

'Maude, I told you already. I will not have you pawning any of your possessions, especially not something you've inherited from your mother. Trust me, I can afford this.' He looked deep into her eyes to try and convince her and she finally relented, lowering her gaze.

'Very well. Thank you, you're very kind.'

The day of the ball dawned fair and the weather held, so they were able to set off without damaging the ladies' delicate silk slippers. Anna was left in the capable hands of Mrs Mason, the cook, although she was allowed to come and wave them off so that she could admire their finery.

Maude knew she looked her best in the beautiful mauve gown that Luke had said suited her colouring, and which was set off by her mother's diamonds. She felt happy for once, and excited about an evening's entertainment. Thomas sent her an appreciative glance, blinking at the sight of her dazzling jewels.

The only fly in the ointment was Eliza, who seemed to be in a sour mood.

'You never told me you had a diamond necklace,' she grumbled, obviously put out because it outshone the amethyst one she had no doubt hoped to show off with. 'And should you really be wearing colours? You have not been widowed for very long.'

'You will have to blame me, I am afraid,' Luke put in. 'It was I who insisted on a bit of colour. Black or grey is so boring.'

'Besides, we will be among friends – so I do not think anyone will mind me wearing mauve just this once,' Maude added, annoyed that Eliza was attempting to ruin things. She had only been widowed just over a year herself and was wearing an outfit of bright pink – which incidentally did not go at all well with the amethysts.

'Perhaps you are right, although you know the tabbies will always talk,' Eliza replied airily, and Maude could tell she was still out of sorts.

Sir Henry and Lady Wallace received them at the entrance to the ballroom, both singling Maude out for special attention.

'My dear, how lovely to see you out and about at last.' Sir Henry defied convention and kissed her soundly on both cheeks. 'Past time you were enjoying yourself again. Are you well? I heard about the accident.'

'I am fine, thank you. I have a hard head.' She smiled at him.

'Well, you take care of yourself, my dear. We would not want any harm to come to you. Is that not so, eh, Hexham?' Sir Henry turned to his other guests, as if finally remembering their presence.

Maude saw Eliza frown again, but there was nothing she could do to appease her. Sir Henry had always had a soft spot for Maude and treated her like the daughter he had never had.

'Indeed, sir,' Luke replied. 'We are taking good care of her, and I have the carriage and horses carefully checked before we go any-where.'

'Good, good, glad to hear it. In you go, then – the musicians are just striking up the first tune.'

As they entered the ballroom, a footman stood just inside the doors handing out dance cards. Eliza wasted no time in holding hers out to Luke. 'I might as well ask you to sign this now,' she said. 'No doubt you will soon be besieged, so it is my only chance. Oh, and you too, Mr Hexham,' she added as an afterthought to Thomas. Both gentlemen scrawled their names on her card, but Maude noticed they only claimed one dance each.

'Are you not dancing, Maude?' Luke asked, looking at her hands which were holding nothing but her reticule and a fan.

She shook her head. 'No – it is too soon. I would not want the tabbies to gossip too much. As Eliza said, I will give them more than enough to talk about by wearing this gown.'

Luke glanced at Eliza, who was busy scanning the room for other likely dance partners, but he only said, 'I see. Can I fetch you a glass of champagne at least?'

'Thank you, yes, that would be lovely.'

Luke did his duty and danced with just about every eligible young lady in the room, as well as all the wallflowers. He had always wondered why other men did not take the trouble to at least dance with the dowdier girls. Even if they did not wish to marry them, the effort required was always repaid a hundredfold by the gratitude in the ladies' eyes.

There was only one woman he really wanted to lead onto the floor, however, and she spent the evening sitting in a corner with some tedious matrons. But even hidden away like that, she drew his gaze, time and again.

He gathered from snippets of conversation he overheard that everyone was pleased to welcome Maude back. From what he could understand, she had barely socialised at all during the last few years and everywhere he went, he heard veiled comments about Edward's mistreatment of her.

'A right shame, carrying on like that when you have a diamond of the first water waiting for you at home.'

'She never complained enough, held her head high…'

'And well she should. Wasn't her fault now, was it?'

And so it went on. Luke began to realise that she was well-liked and respected and could not possibly be the heartless liar he had tried to build up in his mind. It made him wonder even more why she had chosen Edward instead of him, because it simply didn't make sense. He could not ask her, though; he had his pride. If she had wanted to marry him, she would have kept their assignation. He would love to know why she had changed her mind; perhaps if he spent more time with her, he would find out eventually.

To that aim, he went to seek her out.

'Lady Hexham, you are looking pale. Would you care to take a turn about the terrace?'

Maude looked up and found Luke standing in front of her, with his hand held out as if he knew she would not refuse. She felt her cheeks heat up, but the ladies she had been talking to were all fanning themselves and seemed not to notice. It was awfully warm in the ballroom, after all.

'I … yes, thank you, that would be most

pleasant.' She stood up and took his arm. Very soon, they were out on a wide, stone-paved terrace, lit only by a few randomly placed lanterns. To her surprise, there was no one else there and she could only surmise everyone was dancing.

The music could still be heard through the open French windows and Maude noticed the orchestra strike up a waltz. Before she had time to comment on this, Luke took her in his arms and began to dance with her, his steps in perfect tune with the lilting melody.

'Luke!' she protested, using his given name without thinking. 'No, really, I shouldn't...' But her feet had begun to move of their own accord, her body following gracefully.

'Hush, no one will see us here.' His voice was low, soothing, and she allowed herself to be seduced by the feeling of being in his arms, twirling the way they'd done so often that wonderful summer eight years previously.

Neither of them said anything until the music came to an end. Maude found that by then, they were at the far end of the terrace in virtual darkness and there was still no one else outside. Although he had stopped dancing, Luke did not let her go. In the faint light of the full moon, she saw his eyes searching hers for a moment, and felt her own widen. She did not know what he was looking for, nor whether he found it, but in the next instant he bent his head and captured her lips in a delicate kiss.

So soft was his mouth on hers, that at first it was a mere whisper of skin on skin, but he didn't stop there. When she did not move or protest, he deepened the kiss and her traitorous mouth returned it in full measure. She remembered all too clearly how wonderful it felt to be kissed by Luke and she responded without thinking.

This was what she had longed for – this felt right.

He pulled her closer and she felt his heart beating against hers. She inhaled the scent of him, so achingly familiar, stirring up memories best forgotten. A part of her knew she should break away from him and run back to the safety of the ballroom, but her limbs refused to obey. This was where she wanted to be. This was heaven.

An almighty crash made them spring apart and Maude heard Luke swearing under his breath while he hopped on one leg. 'Hell and damnation,' he muttered. 'What on earth...?'

He looked at a broken plant pot lying on the ground only inches away from where they had been standing. It had shattered into a thousand pieces, which were scattered all around together with the soil and a few bits of roots and leaves. Luke scowled and stared upwards, scanning the roof line as if searching for evidence of some sort.

'Wh-where did that come from?' Maude stammered, then noticed a gash in Luke's trousers. 'Your leg! Are you hurt?'

'Yes, but it is nothing – a mere scratch. A shard must've gone into my skin.' He seemed unconcerned and continued to scan the roof above them. 'This has gone beyond a joke, though. I shall not tolerate this any longer.'

'Tolerate what?' Maude blinked at him in confusion.

'These so-called accidents. There have been too many now for them to be mere coincidences. Someone is trying to do away with one of us and I intend to catch the culprit. I won't stand for it.'

'They are t-trying to k-kill us?' Maude found that she was shivering uncontrollably now and Luke must have noticed because he shrugged out of his jacket and draped it round her shoulders.

'Do not worry,' he murmured. 'I will not let anyone hurt you ever again. I shall get to the bottom of this matter, never fear. Come, let me take you inside. Perhaps there is a room where you can lie down for a moment.'

'I do not want to rest, I am fine.' She put a hand on his arm. 'Please do not do anything rash. You might be hurt.'

He stopped and gazed into her eyes. 'Do you care?'

Maude drew in a harsh breath, but looked

away. 'Of course. You are … family,' she mumbled.

'Family? Is that all I am?' He waited a moment, as if he expected her to look at him again, but she could not without giving away the feelings that were rushing through her.

'Well, I … yes, but…' She could not get the words out – could not tell him how she really felt. He probably still despised her, and after the way she had just melted into his arms, what must he think of her? She was supposed to be mourning his cousin and here she was, allowing him liberties.

But she was so afraid for him, so scared of losing him again. Even if she could not have him herself, she wanted him to be alive. The alternative did not bear thinking about.

He gave her another searching look, but gave her no further chance to explain what she meant.

'Let us rejoin the party,' he said. He put his arm around her waist and propelled her towards the doors. 'I want you somewhere safe.'

CHAPTER NINE

Luke was wrong, and his 'mere scratch' turned out to need stitching. He refused to allow Maude to send for a doctor, however, and insisted on having Stetson perform the necessary procedure.

'He has done this before and I trust him,' was his explanation and Maude could see that he meant it. They had been through so much together in the Peninsula, she guessed this was not the first time either of them had needed such treatment.

'Very well,' she agreed, 'but please let me bandage your leg when he has finished. I'll bring the necessary linen.'

Luke submitted to her ministrations once Stetson had done his part. 'I have to admit you've a lighter touch,' he managed to joke, although she was sure she must be hurting him every time the bandage came into contact with his torn skin. He was so pale; she wanted to wrap her arms around him and kiss him again until he forgot about the pain.

The short interlude on the terrace had been heaven – and at the same time, sheer torture because she was sure the kiss had only been a moment of madness and he had meant nothing by it. But now she longed for him to take her in his arms and do it again.

She concentrated on her task so that he would not see her overheated cheeks at these inappropriate thoughts. 'Stetson seems like a good man,' she ventured, hoping a normal conversation would help her keep her composure. 'Were you always in the same regiment?'

'Yes, I met him on my very first day and we have rarely been apart since. We fought together on many occasions and there is no one I would rather have watching my back. I owe him my life.'

Maude was sure Stetson probably owed Luke his as well, but Luke was too modest to say so. She admired his loyalty and knew that whoever won his trust and affection would have it for life – unless they betrayed him.

That was obviously what he thought she'd done, and she had no idea how to convince him that it wasn't true.

Would he listen to her if she tried, or was it entirely too late? Could she find a way to explain? It was a faint hope but she knew she would cling to it for as long as possible.

'Mama? Can I go and see the kittens again?'

Maude looked up from the household accounts, which she had been adding up. She was pleased to see that it all tallied and she was looking forward to showing them to Luke. He had given her funds to replenish the stores of food in the larder, and she had managed to do so and still have some money left over. She hoped he would be pleased.

'The kittens? Yes, I don't see why not. Just be careful, dear, they have such sharp little claws.'

As Anna skipped out of the room, Maude

realised she should have asked who Anna was going with, but assumed Mrs Mason was taking her. The kittens were only in one of the stables, after all, so it was not as if they were far away. Anna would be fine.

She picked up the accounts and went in search of Luke.

'Dash it all, I am not an invalid! There is no reason why I should stay in bed on such a fine day just because of a few stitches in my leg. I can still ride, and let the horse do all the walking.'

'Very well, my lord, but do not blame me if you tear the wound open.'

Stetson left the room with a distinct sniff and Luke glared after him. The man may be the best of fellows, but sometimes he took too much upon himself. The leg was healing just fine and after three days of boredom, nothing on earth could keep Luke cooped up in his bedroom. He picked up a cane that Stetson had left for him just to humour the man, and made his way downstairs. He refused to acknowledge that the pain was any more than bearable whenever he put his weight on the left leg. That would have been tantamount to admitting defeat.

As he reached the bottom step, Maude came towards him carrying a sheet of paper. Her expression changed from one of contentment to instant alarm at the sight of him.

'Should you be up and about?' she asked, glancing at his injured limb.

'Not you as well,' he groaned. 'Why will no one trust my judgement? If I was on my deathbed, I'd damn well stay in my room, but as I am not, I have work to do.'

Maude's lips twitched as if she was hiding a smile, but all she said was, 'Very good, my lord. Then perhaps I should show you the accounts later?'

'No, by all means, bring them along now.'

He managed to limp as far as the estate office and sank down onto the chair with a secret sigh of relief. Perhaps he had been somewhat hasty in leaving his bed, but he was here now – and the sight of Maude made him forget the pain.

She was looking particularly lovely today in one of the new gowns he had ordered for her. Although it was dark grey, it was embroidered at the hem, cuffs and neckline with silver flowers which shimmered in the sunlight streaming in through the window. He reflected that she would probably look good even dressed in rags, but he enjoyed seeing her in clothes that enhanced her beauty.

'Are you listening to me?' Maude's voice interrupted his thoughts.

'I beg your pardon? So sorry, I was just thinking about something. What were you saying?'

'I was just explaining about these two entries here…'

Luke tried to pay more attention, but every time his gaze fell on her mouth, he could not help but remember the kiss they had shared on the Wallaces' terrace. A kiss that probably should not have happened, but which he could not regret. He was no nearer to solving the mystery of her marriage to Edward, but he did know now that she was not indifferent to him. Far from it.

'Lord Hexham, are you sure you should not be in bed? It seems to me you are still under the influence of laudanum.'

'What? Oh, yes, perhaps you are right.' Luke thought it was probably better if she thought him hazy because of the sleeping draught. If she had any inkling of the real reason for his distraction, she would in all likelihood leave the room.

'Should I ask Cook to prepare you some coffee, perhaps? Or would you like to return to…'

'No! I am not going upstairs and that's final.'

She held up her hands. 'Very well, my lord. I shall go and see about the coffee, then.'

Maude could not find any servants about and decided it was probably faster if she went to the kitchen herself. There she found Mrs Mason busy chopping vegetables and ordering the scullery maid about.

'His lordship would like some coffee in the

estate office, please,' Maude requested, then remembered Anna. 'So you have returned from looking at the kittens, then?'

'Kittens?' Mrs Mason looked puzzled. 'I don't have time to look at no kittens today, my lady. Besides, I already chose the one I want.'

'Oh – but I thought Anna was going there again with you. Who was she with, then?'

'I'm sure I could not say, my lady. She came through here earlier, but as far as I remember, she was on her own.'

A stirring of unease rippled through Maude. 'Hmm, perhaps I had better go and have a look for her. She can't have gone far. The kittens are in the far stable, am I right?'

'Yes, that's the one.'

Maude headed out the back door and went straight to the farthest stable, where she found one of the stable lads feeding the cat and her little ones. There was no sign of Anna.

'Ah, Josh, did you see where Miss Anna went?'

'No, my lady. She's not been here today so I'm sure I couldn't tell yer where she might be.'

'What, not at all?'

Josh shrugged. 'No, ma'am. Haven't seen 'er since day afore yesterday.'

'Oh, dear.' Maude felt her heart begin a tattoo of apprehension.

'Is something wrong, my lady?'

Maude shook her head. 'No, no – it's probably nothing.'

'Sorry I can't help yer.'

Maude thanked him and went back outside. Soon she had asked just about every groom in sight, but no one had seen hide nor hair of Anna. The child's sturdy pony was still in its stable, and when Maude checked with the gardeners, they had not seen her daughter either. Panic was starting to squeeze her insides, and she returned to the estate office.

'Luke, I cannot find Anna,' she blurted out – forgetting to address him by his title, so great was her apprehension now.

He put down the cup of coffee he had just finished and frowned. 'What do you mean? She is lost?'

Maude explained what had happened and saw his brows come down in an almighty frown. 'Damn it all,' he muttered. 'Where is Mrs Gascombe? Could she be with her?'

'No. She has had to return to her own house today to sort out some estate matters.'

'Thomas?'

'Went fishing ages ago and has not come back yet.'

'Right, well, let's organise a search party. She is probably just hiding somewhere in the house, playing at hide and seek or some such thing. Let's not worry yet. She will turn up, you'll see.'

But after an exhaustive search of the house and grounds, there was still no sign of Anna. It was as if she had disappeared into thin air.

Maude sat in the parlour by herself, forcing down a cup of tea and some cake. She barely tasted it and was having trouble swallowing, but she knew she had to make herself eat. If she did not keep her strength up, she would be no use to anyone. And she had to remain strong so that she could find her daughter.

Luke was heading the search outdoors, and she trusted him to see that no stone remained unturned. She was determined to join him and the other people who had been recruited from the village to help with the search as soon as she'd finished. She could not rest until Anna had been found.

Guilt streaked through her. She should have paid more attention earlier when Anna came to tell her what she was up to. Maude was mortified to remember that the only thing she had been able to think about all the time was how much she was looking forward to seeing Luke and talking to him about the accounts. About anything, since she grasped at every excuse just to be in the same room as him.

It was madness.

Just because he had kissed her once did not mean he wanted to rekindle their relationship. He probably still thought her a heartless deceiver and had only kissed her because she was there, available. Or perhaps to punish her. For punishment it surely was – the scene played inside her head over and over again until she wanted to scream with frustration. She had been on the verge of asking him so many times what he had meant by it, but could not make herself utter the words.

He had probably just been toying with her.

And now Anna was gone, and it was all her fault. She was a thoroughly bad mother, thinking only of herself. *Dear God, please don't let any harm come to her! She is only little. Where on earth could she be?*

Maude's thoughts were interrupted by the entrance of Donne with a stack of letters. 'Thank you, just put them there,' she said, hardly noticing.

Donne did as he'd been asked, but kept one letter back which he held out to her. 'I think perhaps you ought to read this one, my lady,' he said, his expression grave and his eyes full of concern.

'What?' Maude glanced at the proffered letter and froze momentarily. On the outside was printed in large letters, *TO LADY HEXHAM – URGENT.* Maude snatched it out of Donne's hand and tore it open.

One of a pair of new hair ribbons that Luke had bought for Anna fell out, and Maude gasped and caught it. Her stomach clenched with terror when she realised Anna had been wearing them that morning, and she had to blink to clear her vision so that she could read the accompanying note.

The child is safe for now. Bring your diamond necklace to Hope Spring tonight at midnight. Leave it under the large oak tree and go back to wait by the road. The child will be delivered to you there if you do as we say. Do not tell a soul, and come alone, or else you will never see the child alive again.

'Bad news, my lady?' Donne enquired gently.

Maude shook her head and tried to paste a false smile on her face.

'N-no. Everything is f-fine. You may go.'

Donne hesitated as if he did not believe her, but it was not his place to question his mistress. He bowed. 'Very good, my lady.'

Luke felt fear gripping his insides tighter and tighter for every hour that passed. He had been helping with the search for Anna, but as far as he could see, they had now exhausted all possible hiding places. He went back to the house to report this disappointing news to Maude, although he hoped against hope that the child would have turned up in the meantime.

He was met at the door by Donne, who immediately told him about the letter Maude had just received.

'An urgent letter, you say? Hmm, yes, I have to agree it does sound highly suspicious.'

'Indeed, my lord – my thoughts precisely, which is why I thought it my duty to inform you.'

Luke nodded. 'Thank you, Donne, you did the right thing. I shall speak to her ladyship immediately.'

He found her standing immobile by a window, staring into the garden without really seeing it. 'Maude?' he said and laid a hand gently on her arm. 'Maude, how are you bearing up?'

She turned slowly, her blue eyes filled with anguish, then quickly lowered her gaze. Taking a deep breath, she straightened her shoulders.

'I am … fine, thank you. As well as can be expected, at any rate.'

He shook his head.

'Surely you do not expect me to believe that? I know you too well. Has something else happened?'

'I … don't know what you mean.' She turned away from him and pretended to stare out the window again.

'Maude.' There was a warning note in his voice. Did she really think she could deceive him? She ought to know him better than that.

She bent her head and put her arms

around herself, as if the pain inside her was too much to bear. 'I am not supposed to tell you,' she whispered hoarsely. 'Anna ... I cannot jeopardise...'

'Nonsense,' he said firmly. 'Besides, you do not have to tell me anything; just show me the letter you received. I'll wager that will explain it.'

'Letter?' She blinked at him.

'The ever-efficient Donne told me. Nothing escapes him. Now if you let me read it, you will not have physically said anything to anyone, right?'

He saw a flush of something like amusement at his subterfuge, but it was gone from her eyes as quickly as it had appeared. She produced the letter from her pocket without quibbling, however, and it did not take him long to read. He swore under his breath.

'They are not going to get away with this. I shall go and speak to the magistrate myself,' he growled.

'No! No, you mustn't!' Maude cried, clearly agitated. 'Do you not understand?

They will kill her. My little girl…' Tears spilled over, but she dashed them away and stared at him beseechingly. 'Please, Luke. We cannot tell anyone.'

'But the kidnappers would never know. I will go in secret.'

'We cannot be sure of that. What if they are having us watched? What if someone is listening to us even now? Then they will know I did not keep the matter to myself, and Anna…'

He shook his head. 'I think we are safe indoors, but you may be right. They knew about your necklace, so they must have been watching you closely. Wait, I must think.'

He began to pace the room unevenly, leaning on his cane, thinking hard. There had to be some way of rescuing Anna, while still apprehending the culprits and retaining Maude's necklace.

Any alternative scenario made his blood run cold and simply did not bear thinking of.

CHAPTER TEN

'Listen to me. We are going to tell everyone that Anna is with Mrs Gascombe and that you have just received a note to that effect. Anna had forgotten to ask your permission, while Mrs Gascombe assumed that she had. She has only just found out, and has let you know the child is safe.'

Luke had stopped his pacing at last and was outlining his plan to Maude. She hung on his every word, because her brain felt paralysed and she was sure she couldn't have thought of anything sensible herself. She nodded.

'That news will hopefully filter through to the abductors,' he continued, 'and they will think you have not told anyone. In this way, we will not jeopardise Anna's life by not complying with the instructions. Let us pretend the note informed you that they have decided that Anna is to spend the night at Holby Manor.'

Maude nodded again distractedly, but then protested, 'She has never been away from home before.'

'Then she would find it an adventure, perhaps, although we can let it be known that Mrs Gascombe is not very pleased with this turn of events,' Luke commented drily. 'Everyone must know by now what her views on children are.'

Maude tried to smile. 'Yes, indeed – but Anna is an expert at getting her own way. We can say she must have twisted Eliza's arm somehow.'

'Hmm, to be sure – but will Eliza help us by agreeing to this pretence without a proper explanation, do you think?'

'I do not think there is any need to inform her. Holby is far enough away that hopefully Eliza will not hear about this until tomorrow – and by then, it will all be over, one way or another.' Maude shivered.

'Yes, you are quite right.'

'So you will call off the search now all is supposedly well?'

'Yes. I am certain the men will be pleased. They are all as worried as we are. Little Anna is well liked.' He headed wearily for the door. 'Let me just tell everyone, and then I shall be back to outline the rest of my plan.'

Going to Hope Spring in daylight was one thing, but even thinking about going there in the dead of night was quite another. Maude did not see that she had any choice, however. If she wanted her daughter back, it was something she had to do. The thought of being out and about all by herself might be frightening, but never seeing Anna again was unthinkable.

Besides, she would not be entirely alone. Luke would be there somewhere, in the shadows. He had promised. It was immensely reassuring to know that he was helping her, even if he could not be seen to do so openly. She was very grateful for his support and doubted very much she could have achieved so much on her own.

Before going anywhere, however, she had to endure the long wait until it was time to leave, and the evening seemed interminable. Maude found that that having to make small talk with only Luke and Thomas, without Eliza's usual chatter enlivening the conversation, was absolute purgatory. Luke did his best to help, but was rather abstracted and answered most questions with monosyllables that made Maude want to scream with frustration. Thomas kept throwing them both strange glances, which Maude had to counter by trying to appear calm and collected. It was a relief to retreat to the salon while they lingered over their port, but her peace was short-lived when they joined her remarkably quickly.

As soon as the tea tray had been removed, Maude excused herself.

'I am sorry, but it has been a somewhat fraught day and I find I am very tired. I bid you goodnight.'

She escaped to her room, but instead of

preparing for bed, she dressed warmly for the hour-long ride to Hope Spring, then paced the room. She was too agitated to lie down and rest, as would have been sensible. The preparations were also managing to set her nerves on edge because they reminded her of that night so long ago when she should have made her escape with Luke.

A shiver hissed down her spine, and she went quickly to check that the door opened freely. This time nothing must go wrong. She had to leave the house, or all would be lost.

Just like last time.

This is different, she told herself. And someone had known of her plans then, whereas they did not now. Just in case, however, she left her door slightly ajar and blocked the keyhole with the corner of a handkerchief so that no one could lock her in. It seemed a silly thing to do, but she was taking no chances. Not this time.

Anna was too precious.

'You do not really believe that story, do

you?' Thomas said as soon as Maude's foot-steps had disappeared upstairs.

Luke had been lost in thought, but these words brought him back to the present with a jolt. 'What story?' he asked, feigning in-comprehension.

Thomas snorted. 'The one about her daughter staying with Mrs Gascombe. It is as plain as day, that annoying woman cannot abide children, so there is no way she would take the little girl with her on an outing, let alone have her to stay the night with her. For some reason, Lady Hexham is bamming us.'

'Well, I...' Luke did not know quite how to answer this. He did not want to tell Thomas outright that he knew it was a lie. He still had not got to the bottom of who was trying to kill either himself or Maude, and since Thomas was one of the prime suspects, he knew it would be utter madness to confide in him.

What if it was in fact Thomas who had abducted Anna and he was merely playing a deep game now? Had Thomas laced

Maude's tea with arsenic, tampered with the carriage or sent that flower pot crashing down next to them on the terrace? It was entirely possible – and he was the only one who had a motive, as far as Luke could see.

Thomas sent him a searching glance, then appeared as though understanding had suddenly dawned.

'Oh, I see,' he said slowly. 'If the child really has disappeared, you think I might have something to do with it, so you're keeping me in the dark? Well, think again. I have spent the entire day with two of the gamekeepers, so I would be in the clear. They will vouch for me, no question.'

'Well, speaking hypothetically, if she was missing, a person does not actually have to be present in order to have her abducted,' Luke pointed out. 'If you were indeed the one responsible, you could have paid someone else to do the job for you. But there is no point discussing this since she is safely at Mrs Gascombe's house.'

'Oh, for Heaven's sake, we both know she is

not. Let's not pretend about that,' Thomas retorted. He glared at Luke. 'I am not stupid, you know – you cannot fool me. And Lady Hexham was on edge the entire evening. I could tell, even though she tried her best to hide it. Now, why would I wish to harm a child? I admit I am not used to dealing with them, but that does not mean I dislike little Anna.'

Luke decided there was no point beating around the bush any longer. 'You tell me. There seem to have been a surprising number of accidents and illnesses around here recently – and the only person who stands to gain anything from hurting me and my relatives is you.'

Thomas's eyes opened wide. 'You think I am trying to kill you so that I will inherit Hexham Hall?'

'Are you not?' Luke countered, fixing Thomas with a piercing gaze.

'No, absolutely not! That is a slanderous suggestion, sir. I came here in good faith to offer my support in your new position, that was all. I did not come here to be insulted and…'

Luke held up a hand. 'Enough. I am not saying that it necessarily has to be you. I have only pointed out that you do have something to gain. No one else does, to my knowledge.'

'Well, it was not me. And I do not need this run-down estate, thank you very much. I am to inherit a substantial holding from an uncle on my mother's side soon, and I can live without a title, I'll have you know.'

Luke could see that Thomas was in earnest. He did not think his cousin could lie if he tried, because his face became suffused with tell-tale colour whenever he was agitated or embarrassed. The same would happen if he lied, Luke was sure.

'I believe you,' he said, and sighed. 'But that does not help me solve the problem of who is really behind these attempts. Any ideas?'

Thomas calmed down when he saw that he was no longer accused of any misdeeds. 'No, afraid not. But I am willing to help you in any way I can.'

'In that case, you can start tonight. You are right, Anna has been abducted and Maude and I have to try and rescue her. A note arrived. We are to go to Hope Spring to pay a ransom. A few more allies would not go amiss and I have already recruited my valet, Stetson, but no one else must know. Are you game?'

'Absolutely.' Thomas nodded emphatically. 'You can count on me.'

'Thank you. Then please pretend to go to bed as usual, but sneak out and meet me down by the stables an hour before midnight. Maude will leave on her own; we will wait and make sure nobody is watching. Then we have to follow her. It is the only way.'

'Sounds like a good plan.'

Luke was not so sure, but it was the best he could come up with. He hoped he was not making a huge mistake in trusting Thomas, but somehow he did not think so.

'Very well. Bring a pistol if you have one, and make sure it's loaded.'

151

At last, it was time to go. Maude put on her hat, gathered up her riding whip and gloves, as well as a small reticule containing the diamond necklace, and tiptoed out into the corridor. All was quiet and as she made her way down the stairs, she could not hear a sound from anywhere in the house.

When she reached the stables, it was just as peaceful. Mayflower greeted her with a snort, but was quickly appeased with a carrot Maude had thought to bring. The horse made no protest when her mistress saddled her, either. Not having been spoiled while growing up, Maude was perfectly able to accomplish the task by herself and had no need to summon the grooms for assistance. This was just as well, she thought, since she did not want anyone to know that she was going out. Mayflower followed her into the night without a murmur.

Anna, here I come, Maude thought. *Nothing must stop me now.* She squared her shoulders and nudged Mayflower into a canter. She knew the way well, and had no doubt she could find the place even with only a half moon for guidance.

Riding through the countryside in near darkness was very strange. With the faint moonlight bathing the trees and hedges in an unearthly glow, Maude felt as if she was in some peculiar dream land. At any moment, she expected to see elves and fairies, or even trolls and goblins, come lumbering out of a nearby copse of trees. The thought sent fresh shivers down her spine and she tightened her hands on the reins until the leather was digging into her palms.

A barn owl made her jump when it hooted nearby and then flitted past her, like a ghostly shadow. Maude felt her heart beating at double its normal rate and swallowed down the fear that rose within her.

'It is but an owl, he cannot hurt you,' she told herself. She knew she had nothing to fear from the creatures of the night. It was humans who were her real enemies.

Oh, Anna, what have they done to you? She could not stop the thoughts that tormented her with images of Anna suffering at the hands of her abductors. Hopefully they would keep her safe until such time as they had received the ransom – but what if they did not? What if they had hurt her beloved daughter already?

Stop it. Maude admonished herself sternly. Such thoughts would lead to madness and she needed her wits about her now if she was to help her daughter. The abductors would have nothing to gain by hurting anyone – all they cared about were the diamonds. *And they are welcome to them,* Maude thought savagely. The wretched stones had brought her nothing but trouble. Indeed, she was beginning to think they were cursed and it would be a blessed relief to be rid of them.

As she turned right at a crossroads, following the sign that pointed to Hope Spring, she thought she heard hoof beats behind her, but when she stopped to listen all was silent.

She told herself she was just being fanciful. There was no one about except her and possibly Luke – which was as it should be, otherwise there was no hope for Anna.

'How much further to Hope Spring?' Thomas asked in hushed tones when Luke gave him the signal that he was allowed to speak again. For a moment, it had looked as though Maude was on the verge of turning back, and Luke had made them all wait in silence for a while to see what she would do. Thankfully, she soon set off again.

'Another half an hour or so,' Luke replied. 'We are just approaching Bell House, where Maude grew up, which is about halfway along the route.'

The words brought back powerful memories and he had a sense of déjà vu. Not too far from this place, eight years ago, he had walked his horse and the spare one he had hired while waiting for the woman he hoped to make his wife. She had not kept their tryst that time, but now she was riding about the countryside in the dark and he did not like it at all. He had to keep her safe – her and the child both.

'I wonder who will be waiting for her,' Thomas wondered out loud.

'No doubt we shall find out soon enough,' Luke replied. 'We must proceed with caution from now on, though. I think it would be best if we tether our horses some way off and walk the last stretch.'

'Stetson, I have a bad feeling about this. Could you ride to fetch Sir Henry Wallace, please? He is the local magistrate. We may have need of him, I fear.'

'Are you sure, my lord? I thought we had to keep this matter to ourselves.'

'Yes, but by the time he arrives, it will not be a secret any longer.'

'But what if you require my help here?' Stetson had not been so convinced as Luke that Thomas was innocent of all wrong-doing. He also knew that Luke's wound was troubling him, although Luke had en-deavoured to play this down.

'No, we shall be fine. Off you go.'

'Very well, if you say so.' Stetson frowned in Thomas's direction one last time, then took the road to the left which led to Wallace House.

Luke looked at Thomas. 'Right – are you ready?'

Thomas nodded. 'Lead the way.'

CHAPTER ELEVEN

Hope Spring was really nothing more than a small waterfall that gushed its way down a slope and formed a tiny pool surrounded by rocks. It was rather a picturesque spot in daylight, which was why it was regarded as such a choice destination for a pleasure outing. In the moonlight, however, it looked eerie and the endless cascade of water sounded loud in the stillness of the night.

Maude shivered as she jumped down from Mayflower's back and held on tight to the reins. Somehow the horse felt solid and safe, something to cling onto. Mayflower must have felt her mistress's shaking hands, for she nudged Maude softly and whinnied.

'I know, girl, I know,' Maude whispered soothingly. 'You like this not a jot more than I do, do you? Let's just leave this blasted necklace of mine, and then we may go.'

There was only one large oak tree in the vicinity as far as Maude could see, and she made her way over to it as quickly as she could. A prickling between her shoulder blades gave her the feeling she was being watched, but she tried not to let this daunt her.

Pulling the reticule containing the diamond necklace out of her pocket, she put it down among the gnarled roots of the old tree. She made sure it was clearly visible since she wanted it to be found immediately.

'There, Mayflower, it's done,' she breathed, turning away. 'Let's go back to the road and wait, then...'

'Not so fast.'

The voice that rang out suddenly startled both Maude and the mare, and Maude swivelled round to see where it had come from. Standing by the spring, she made out three figures, one smaller than the others and struggling slightly as if trying to evade a strong grip.

'Anna!' Maude could not prevent the anguished cry from escaping her lips, but then clamped her teeth together so as not to say anything else until she knew what was happening.

Anna made only muffled noises, which made Maude realize, to her shock, that the little girl was gagged. She wanted to hurl herself across the clearing and go immediately to her daughter's aid, but one of the other two figures held something in his or her hand that glimmered in the moonlight – a knife.

'Come no closer or the girl dies.'

The same voice as before – that of a man, deep and harsh. Maude did not recognise it and it caused a tremor of fear to shoot through her.

The third figure moved forward and as it came closer, something about it seemed familiar. Maude frowned, then she realised why.

'Eliza!' she exclaimed. 'What on earth...? Why are you here? What is going on?'

Eliza stopped a few yards away from Maude, pointing a small pistol at her former friend. 'Always the same innocent, gullible Maude,' she sneered. 'It is as plain as a pike-staff, is it not? I need your diamond necklace if I am to make a good marriage this time. His lordship will not marry a penniless widow, now, will he? And contrary to what everyone thinks, I haven't a feather to fly with.'

'H-his lordship? You mean ... *Luke?*' Maude was thoroughly confused now. She had of course noticed Eliza flirting with Luke whenever she had the opportunity, but she had not realised the woman was in deadly earnest.

After all, why would Luke settle for a widow when he could have his pick of all the eligible young ladies in the neighbourhood?

Unless, perhaps, he did not wish to wait so

long until the estate was prosperous again, and needed to obtain money quickly...

'Of course I mean Luke,' Eliza snapped. 'He should have been mine in the first place, but you had to come and interfere. I met him that spring, when you were away visiting your relatives in Hertfordshire, and we were well on the way to an understanding. The minute he set eyes on you, however, I was forgotten. I could not put up with that.'

Maude frowned. 'What are you saying? You tried to stop Luke from marrying me?'

Eliza laughed, although it was a sound without mirth. 'I did not just try, I succeeded. A quick word in the ear of your father's valet, and you were trapped. He locked you in, did he not, the night you were going to elope? It was I who told him to. Hah!'

Maude felt her eyes fill with tears, but she dashed them away and drew in a deep breath. All these years of misery she had endured – and only because Eliza had been jealous. It did not bear thinking of.

At the same time the knowledge made

Maude furious, giving her strength, and she gritted her teeth against the pain. She would not think about that now; she had to concentrate on getting Anna back. That was the only thing that mattered, not the past.

'Fine – take the necklace. You are welcome to it. Just give me back my daughter.'

'Oh, you can have her all right. Go and join her, by all means. You and she are about to embark on a little journey with my partner in crime over there, Mr Hampton.'

'Journey? What do you mean?' Maude felt icy fingers of terror gripping her insides. 'And who is he?'

'Mr Hampton is the man my late husband – may he rot in hell – played his final game of cards with. Unfortunately, Gascombe lost and Mr Hampton has been plaguing me for settlement of the debt. Since Gascombe Park is already mortgaged to the hilt and I am as poor as a church mouse, that is where you come in. You and your pretty bauble. It is a shame I did not know you owned it before you wore it to that ball. Then I could have stolen the necklace and no one would have been any the wiser.'

'But…' Maude's thoughts were whirling.

'For pity's sake, stop asking so many questions. Go to your precious child and do whatever it is mothers do. You do not have much time.'

Maude began to shake, but after one last dagger look at Eliza, she made her way over to Anna. The little girl looked tiny next to Mr Hampton, who at close quarters turned out to be a huge man with fists the size of hams. His knife still glittered menacingly in the moonlight, but without so much as glancing at him, Maude dropped to her knees in front of her daughter and gave her a quick hug before reaching up to untie the gag.

'Sweetheart, I'm so sorry,' she whispered. 'Are you hurt?'

Anna shook her head, but a sob escaped the little girl nonetheless. It was clear the child was terrified, her wide gaze overflowing with tears.

Mr Hampton did not prevent Maude

from loosening Anna's bonds, so she continued with the cord that bound the child's wrists together. Once she had her free, she rubbed at the sore little arms and then enveloped her in her embrace again.

'Very touching,' Mr Hampton commented with a sneer, then shouted over abruptly to Eliza. 'Have you got it? I do not wish to stand around out here all night.'

'Yes – and these should fetch a tidy sum.' Eliza held up the necklace and Maude saw the stones sparkling faintly.

'Well, what are you waiting for then? Let's be on our way.'

'Hold on a moment. You will not receive your share until you have done away with those two. That was the deal.'

'And what if I have changed my mind? There is no reason why I should risk my neck for your sake. You are the one who wants them dead. All I want is what is owing to me. Now give that here, and I'll break it in half.'

'On no account! Are you mad? I'll have you know...'

While Eliza and her accomplice continued to argue, Maude took her chance and grabbed Anna by the hand. She inched away from Mr Hampton, heading in the direction of a nearby thicket of bushes, but she had gone only a few yards when Eliza spotted them.

'Maude! Do not even think of escaping,' she shouted savagely. 'Stop exactly where you are, or I will surely shoot one of you.'

Maude froze, but in the next instant another voice rang out – one which was far more welcome to Maude's ears.

'No, you will not – or I shall shoot you. And unlike you, I should not think I would miss. I am accounted an excellent shot.'

'Lord Hexham! What are you doing here?' Eliza turned an accusing glare on Maude. 'I told you quite clearly in the letter I sent not to bring anyone with you, you fool.'

'I did not. I mean to say, I truly thought I was alone.'

'We followed Maude without her know-ledge,' Luke lied.

'*We?*' Eliza glanced around wildly, her face a mask of fury.

'Yes, we.' Thomas's voice rang out as he and Luke both stepped out into the clearing. 'I should have known that you were not to be trusted. Anyone who treats servants as badly as you do, madam, is not worthy of being called a lady.'

'Well, here's a fine kettle of fish,' Mr Hampton muttered. 'I've had enough of this.' Without further ado, he reached forward to snatch the diamond necklace out of Eliza's hands and then made a run for it. His sharp whistle brought a pair of horses trotting out from under the nearby trees, and Hampton vaulted onto one of them with surprising agility for someone of his considerable size.

Luke rushed after him, although limping badly which slowed him down. He shouted over his shoulder at Thomas, 'Watch her!' Thomas obeyed, pointing his pistol firmly at Eliza, who still had hers trained on Maude.

'I am faster than you,' Thomas warned, 'so even if you manage to pull the trigger, your shot will go wide and you will have died for nothing.'

Eliza seemed to consider this for a moment, before giving up on the idea of shooting Maude with an angry noise.

Meanwhile, Luke was trying to follow Hampton, who seemed to be getting away. Luke stopped suddenly, knelt on the ground and took careful aim. A shot rang out and in the next instant, Hampton toppled off the horse, hitting the ground with a dull thud.

'I say, capital shot, coz,' Thomas crowed, but Luke did not reply. Instead, he took off again, but just as he reached Hampton, the man got to his feet and started laying about him with those meaty fists. Maude gasped in terror, but from what she could make out in the moonlight, Luke was giving as good as he got.

While Thomas had been distracted momentarily by Luke's endeavours, Eliza took her chance and sprinted towards the remaining horse. She managed to drag herself onto its back and kicked it into a gallop.

Thomas swore under his breath and tried to copy his cousin's previous manoeuvre – kneeling down and taking careful aim, he fired off a shot. Eliza was moving too fast, however, and the bullet went wide.

'Hell and damnation,' Thomas muttered, but although he had missed Eliza, he must have frightened her horse because it began bucking. Eliza tried to hang on for dear life, but the horse was not having any of it. It continued its mad dance until the rider was unseated, and then took off at a panicked gallop.

Unfortunately for Eliza, she still had one foot stuck in a stirrup and Maude could only watch in horror as her former friend was dragged along, screaming, behind the horse before her foot finally became disentangled.

Eliza's lifeless body came to a halt and Maude shuddered – but there was still Luke to worry about. His fight with Hampton was continuing unabated and neither man showed any sign of giving up.

'How can Luke possibly withstand

punches from such enormous fists?' Maude wondered out loud. 'And wounded as he is, too. Go and help him, Thomas, I beg you!'

'Never fear, he is younger and a lot more agile even in his present state,' Thomas replied, but set off towards the two combatants nonetheless. Just before he reached them, however, another shot rang out and he stopped.

Maude did not know whence it had come at first, but then she saw Hampton slump to the ground, while Luke stood panting over him.

She grabbed Anna's hand and they rushed towards him.

'Luke? Luke, are you all right?'

'I am fine,' he panted.

'What happened?' Maude looked from him to Hampton and back. She was just so relieved to see Luke in one piece, she wanted so much now to throw her arms around him, but of course she could do no such thing. She had to be content with touching his arm, just to convince herself he was relatively unharmed.

'He had a pistol hidden in his boot. Tried to fire it, but I managed to turn it. Shot himself by mistake.' Luke bent over, putting his hands on his knees for support. 'I never meant for that to happen.'

'Brought it on himself,' Thomas said philosophically, 'just as the Gascombe woman did.'

'Eliza is dead too?' Luke straightened up and looked in the direction Thomas pointed.

'Seems that way. The horse bolted.'

'Dear Lord, what a mess.'

A sudden commotion nearby heralded the arrival of Stetson with Sir Henry Wallace. The magistrate was quickly apprised of the situation and took control.

'Nothing to worry about,' he said firmly. 'Plenty of witnesses here to verify these were both accidental deaths. I would suggest you take Maude and the little one home now, Hexham, and send for the doctor. I should think they have both had a severe shock.'

Luke nodded. 'Thank you, Sir Henry, we

will do that. Thomas, can you round up the two extra horses, please? Let us be on our way.'

Safely back at Hexham Hall, they took turns to have a hot bath, since heating the water took a while. Everyone apart from Thomas, who went straight to bed, yawning hugely.

'I do not have the appearance of someone dragged through a hedge backwards like the rest of you,' he said, 'but I am definitely in need of my bed. I am glad everyone is safe and sound, especially you, young lady.' Thomas smiled at Anna, and Maude realised he had become used to having a child around and no longer minded her presence.

'I'll beat you at cards yet, just you wait,' Anna replied with spirit, before being marched off to have her bath.

Once Maude had seen her daughter safely put to bed, she had a long soak herself, but afterwards she felt strangely restless. She decided that perhaps a very small measure of brandy could be justified after so many nasty shocks, and to that end she made her way to the library.

As she opened the door, however, she came face to face with Luke, who must have had the same idea.

'Maude? I thought you were asleep.' He was holding the brandy decanter, but put it down and came towards her. 'Are you all right?'

'Yes, I just... I thought perhaps some brandy would help me sleep, but maybe it is not such a good idea. I am sorry, I did not mean to disturb you.'

He stopped in front of her and put out a hand to cup her cheek.

'You disturb me constantly,' he said with a wry smile, 'but not in the way that you mean.'

'I ... I do?' Maude looked into his eyes and tried to read his expression. She saw tenderness, and perhaps something else, something she had not dared hope for.

'How?' she whispered, barely able to get the word out because her heart was hammering so hard within her chest.

'I think you already know that,' he replied and bent his head to give her a soft kiss. 'Your very nearness drives me mad, just as it did eight years ago. It always will, but I would not have it any other way.'

'But I thought...'

'We both know now why you never kept our assignation. I heard what Eliza said.' He put his arms around her and pulled her close. 'I was a fool, Maude, I should have realised you would never let me down voluntarily. But when my uncle told me you had chosen Edward and the title instead, I believed him and my pride was wounded. I had no idea he was in collusion with your father, and that you had nothing to do with it.'

'Oh, Luke, I wanted to come to you so much, but I was locked in and there was no way out. I could not even knot my sheets together to climb out the window. It was too far to the ground. You have no idea...'

He kissed her forehead, her eyelids, her nose, her cheek and she gave a little sigh of contentment.

'There is no point thinking about it any more,' Luke murmured. 'It is in the past. But there is still the future. Will you share that with me? Will you marry me – but in the parish church this time, not in some smithy across the Scottish border?'

She smiled up at him and twined her hands round his neck, pulling his head down for a proper kiss.

'Yes – of course – I cannot think of anything I would rather do,' she murmured ecstatically. 'It is something I have dreamed of every day since you left.'

'And I likewise. I love you, Maude, I always have, I always will – and now I shall gain a daughter as well. What could be more perfect?'

As he sealed their bargain with another passionate kiss, Maude knew that nothing could possibly be more perfect than that.

The publishers hope that this book has given you enjoyable reading. Large Print Books are especially designed to be as easy to see and hold as possible. If you wish a complete list of our books please ask at your local library or write directly to:

Dales Large Print Books
Magna House, Long Preston,
Skipton, North Yorkshire.
BD23 4ND

This Large Print Book, for people
who cannot read normal print,
is published under the auspices of
THE ULVERSCROFT FOUNDATION